THE Shadow THINGS

JENNIFER FREITAG

Jennifer L. Freitag

AMBASSADOR INTERNATIONAL
GREENVILLE, SOUTH CAROLINA & BELFAST, NORTHERN IRELAND

www.ambassador-international.com

THE SHADOW THINGS

Printed in the United States of America

ISBN: 978-1-935507-39-0

Cover Design & Page Layout by David Siglin of A&E Media

AMBASSADOR INTERNATIONAL
Emerald House
427 Wade Hampton Blvd.
Greenville, SC 29609, USA
www.ambassador-international.com

AMBASSADOR BOOKS
The Mount
2 Woodstock Link
Belfast, BT6 8DD, Northern Ireland, UK
www.ambassador-international.com

The colophon is a trademark of Ambassador

To my parents,
the giants on whose shoulders I stand.

Map of Southern Britain

HOOFBEATS OF TIR

THERE WAS A STRONG, HEAVY scent of heather in the air and a purple ranking of clouds above. These were the clear signs of a summer thunderstorm. The ponies in the bramble pens were anxious. There was not a breath of wind anywhere over the Downs; the oak boughs down the southward slopes hung limply and the turf was laid low. Lightning flicked its stallion-tails of light far away over the hills. But the rain did not come; it was as though the clouds were holding their breath; the sensation made one light-headed and oppressed at once.

Indi squatted in a doorway, one of his legs outstretched over the alert form of a hound. Both sets of eyes were upturned to the heavy sky. The hound was brindled like a wolf and was shaped like the wild canine so much that his ancestry was very clear. The young man shifted out of the dun shadows into the dim grey of the early twilight; his features could be seen as sharp and stern, though still clinging to their boyhood. The brows sloped downward over the dark golden eyes, and the thin lips curled back in a low whistle.

"Eh, looks like the first of the summer's storms. What say you, Thern?" he poked the hound.

The scraggly dog turned its eyes from the sky and beat its tail once on the flat, dusty ground. It yawned, snapping it jaws together.

Indi scratched the head that was thrust near him and surveyed the dun-yard of his father the Chieftain's house. The timber and gravel steps ran down before him across the short, level space of dirt before the houseplace. They went between the retainers' quarters where his father's friends and weapon-hounds ate and slept. Then the steps stopped at the wide court at the foot of the hill, around which was set the rest of the steading: the servants' houses, the workers' houses, the byres, and the kennels. Usually it was very busy, especially around suppertime when the young men would be riding in after leaving the mares to guard on the hills, the womenfolk would be going about making the meal, and the children would be screaming and the dogs barking.

But not this evening. It was very quiet this evening, and Indi felt his hackles rise as they always did with the coming of the first summer storms. There was always something very alive about the thunderstorm. Indi shivered and pulled back into the shadows of the doorway, fearful lest the gods of thunder become angry with him—though what he might have done against them, he did not know. The thunder, he knew, was the pounding hooves of Tir, Taranis' horse, and the lightning was the spark of the thunder-god's spear as it rent the heavens. The rain from the thunderstorms was the weeping of the many Taranis had wounded, among them his children and wife, Ancasta.

Twisting his head, Indi looked up at the lintel of the houseplace and saw the ash-white form of Tir carved into the wood. It was a sign of blessing for the household: all under the sign of Tir should be strong and swift and fruitful, both the men and the women, and also the horses and sheep on which the Downspeople made their livelihood.

But the gods were erratic. Even now, across the dun sprawling at his feet with its huddles of women about the doorways and darting bodies of youngsters, Indi could see the wavering blue smudge of smoke rising into the heavy air as the priests burned sacrifices to the gods of thunder in the hopes to appease them, and he knew it would do as much to stop the charge of Tir as a bramble-fence would to stop the flood of the sea.

"You feel it also, the coming of the storm?" a voice suddenly spoke above Indi.

Turning around, the young man looked up at his mother. She was very straight and tall and showed no physical signs that she had borne her noble husband a son and two daughters. Apart from her wise and weathered face, she looked very like a girl who had never been wed to a man. Her eyes were very deep and as green as the sea with tints of gold in them; at present, they were fixed on the dark rows of clouds in the west.

"Yes, Mother, I feel it over strongly." Indi got to his feet and stood by her. Though she was tall, he was taller. His frame nearly filled the doorway, and he had to turn aside to let her see around him. His ruddy hair came down to his tattooed shoulders, but his face was still clean as a boy's; he was still too young to have much of a beard. In a moment he spoke again. "But, it is in my heart that you feel something else."

Tirna, named after the White Horse, took her eyes off the horizon and fixed them instead on her son. There was a tense stretch of silence. Indi gazed back at the tight face before him. She was so beautiful, his mother, but so brittle too. She looked as though he could snap her in half between two of his fingers. Her arms were thin and her body as slender as a reed. How strange it was that she should have such a powerful and bull-like man for a husband as she did.

Tirna broke the silence. "My son, why do you say this?"

Indi looked away at Thern scratching after a beetle in the dust. "Because to you the weather changes now and then and now once more, and for you the only things that matter are the hearthfire burning and the meal cooking and my sisters preparing for their time to be brides. If you should come and stand in the doorway, leaving the pot, to stare at the sky, then surely there must be a reason."

Tirna laughed softly. Her laugh was like the sound of the wind through the beech leaves. She leaned against him as though she were tired and sighed deeply. "I have gone down to the priest several times the past few days," she said. "Do you know why?"

"Because my beautiful mother wishes to become a priestess?" Indi smiled.

Tirna shook her head. "Because I have had strange dreams. In them, the sky grows dark, like this, and the wind drives hard from the west, and in the east a voice cries. I am caught between them. I see Tir against the dark western sky with Taranis arrayed in dark scarlet on his back. They are not distinct; I only see the shadows of them. They are very great and terrible, but the voice in the east, the one that cries, is small. It is brown."

"It is brown, my mother?" Indi frowned now, peering into his mother's face.

"Yes," she said quickly. "Brown. It is small and brown, but it has such a persistent voice! Tir lashes out at it, and Taranis strikes at it with his great spear, both of them great and terrible, but the voice springs up in a thousand other places. Then it isn't brown anymore. It is one colour: a silvery white colour, like the chalk with the sun shining on it." She stopped and looked down at Thern.

"And then what?" Indi asked gently.

"And then I awake," his mother replied.

"Always it is the same?"

"Always."

Indi felt a tingling sensation running through his body. It must have been his dwelling on the dealings of the gods that did it because for one moment he thought the carving of Tir was alive and moving one hoof, blurred and ashen-white. Then he shook his head and cursed himself softly. "What did the priest say?"

Tirna pushed off from him and smoothed out the front of her dress. Resuming her brisk, thoughtful tone, she replied, "He said what he would: the crops would fail, the babies would die. I have heard it all before. It is only the way of things, whether Tir would trample the fields or shed his blessing on them; it is the way of things."

She turned and went back inside without another word, leaving Indi to ponder on what she had said. He looked back at the carving intently, crunching his brows into a frown. It did not move, nor was it blurry. "So?" he dared to ask it. "Is it only the way of things? Do you trample our crops and Karmer the Wolf kill our babies, or is it only the way of things? And who—" he looked first at Thern and then at the purple clouds, "—who determined the way of things?" He stood as if moonstruck for a moment, head tipped to one side. Then, as Thern jumped up and barked when a horse came trotting into the court below, Indi shook himself and said, "No, it is Tir and Taranis and Karmer. Who else would make the way of things?" And with that he called Thern back into the houseplace as the first drops began to spatter the dry earth dark.

The dog came scrabbling, jumping over the threshold and, tripping over the youngest of the household, ran to thrust his head between Indi's knees. He smiled and patted the dog's head. Within, there was a warm stuffiness about the place; the straw rustled underfoot, and the mellow light of the sheep's-fat candles blurred in the smoke of the cooking fire and shone fitfully off the great copper pot in which a thick stew was boiling.

Catching the scent of it, Indi remarked idly, "Thern is hungry."

The oldest of his sisters, Lenag, a younger representation of his mother, turned from the fire and kicked a pile of straw aside. "Thern is always hungry," she replied. "As are you. Shall you be heading to the mens' meat-hall?"

Indi took his thick sealskin cloak off his bed and put it around his shoulders. "I'm going now." He whistled Thern to heel and swung out of the house into the sheets of rain, leaving the womenfolk behind in the houseplace and reverently touching the carving of Tir as he left.

The new rain, blowing across the hills in earnest, caught at him as he began to cross the yard, pummelling him before and behind. His knees were dripping and Thern was a wet mass of fur by the time they ducked in through the low doorway of the meat-hall of his father's warriors. There was a crowd of them before him, the retainers and loyal kinsmen of the Chief. There were around fifty of them in the complex at any one time, but there were others outside the dun that had their own steadings, ready to be called to arms at a lamp-flare from the signal tower or the beating of the hollow copper drum.

Indi ducked into the wide, smoky-golden room and was greeted with the rousing cheers and laughter on all sides. Being the son of the Chief, they were obliged to salute him, but as he was the age of many of them, they were nearly brothers. These were the men he had tumbled with as cubs and lain on the pyres with while their smarting tattoos were pricked into their chests and shoulders. These were the men he had trained with and ridden with and crouched side by side with at foaling time, urging a favourite mare to do her best. He picked out a grouping of them near the middle of the table, one familiar face coming out of the confusion quickest of all. Cynr, as dark as he was fair and of age with him, was his oldest friend and waved as he approached.

"Is it very wet out there?" the young man asked, making room on the bench.

Indi map Matheorex sat down in his place at the table, the long fire at his back, and set his right hand on Thern's head. "It is very wet," he replied. He shook off his shiny sealskin and tossed it to one of the boys to care for. "And I have only come from my father's house."

"So?" said Cynr, tipping his mead horn ominously near to spilling. "I was out in the horse runs a quarter of an hour ago, and the horses were spooked with the thunder-wrack rolling in. Cador and I—" he jerked his thumb at the fellow on his far side, spilling several drops, "—had our hands full picking out the three-year-olds."

Helping himself to his supper, Indi nodded wordlessly. The horses always felt it badly when the summer storms came in.

It was the young man to his right that spoke up next. He was the youngest among them and stood out, for he had a dark complexion and dark eyes with the sun glowing behind them. He was tall for his age, and his nose was curved like an eagle's beak. There were clear markings of Red-Crest blood in him. He drew himself up a little, snatching a glance over his shoulder at the doorway as the thunder murmured like a huge harp above them. "First of the summer storms. Tir will be out tonight."

Indi nodded again, feeling a pale tingle in his flesh. "Indeed. The gods are angry for something. It is the time that Tir ran away with Ancasta."

The old story roused the others. The young warrior Tadc-Hound, much taller than most and very lithe like a wildcat or a fine hunting dog, sat up straighter and turned his darkly maned head and shouted, "Hai, Dser! Sing for us the song of Tir and Ancasta."

Lean, grey old Dser the Bard turned his sightless eyes toward the huddle of young men. There was an uncanniness about his silvery eyes, as though he did see, Indi thought, with that second sight that was familiar to the bard kind. The man's brows sloped downward, furrowing his old brow. For a moment there was silence between them. Then Dser said, "Should I sing this song for you on such a night as this? Surely Taranis would not be pleased with me."

Tadc shook himself and put out a hand, making the sign to avert evil. "Well, perhaps he will overlook your singing it this once."

Glancing down at the spread hand, making the sign himself, Indi was not sure he was so keen on hearing the song. Not on a night like this. Not after his mother's dreams. But Dser shrugged philosophically and shifted toward them, placed his bog-wood harp before him, struck the strings, and began to sing. Sightless though he was, his voice was more beautiful than any male voice the fighting men had ever heard. Jokingly they would call Dser the Lady of the Hall but only until he began to sing. Then all voices stopped and all ears were pricked to listen.

Dser sang of Tir, the noble war god who had once had a man's form as his brother Taranis did. There had been a quarrel between the two of them over the fair goddess Ancasta. Taranis had succeeded in seducing her himself and, enraged, Tir had transformed into a beautiful silver-white horse and invited Ancasta for a ride. The goddess had accepted. Galloping swifter than lightning, Tir leapt across the bounds of the sky and hid himself and his brother's bride among the western clouds. Changing form so swiftly Ancasta hardly knew what was happening, Tir raped her. Her cries echoed through the heavens and Taranis, sitting in his hall, heard her. Furious, he caught up his spear and summoned his sons and hounds to him. They all ran across the sky and tore apart the clouds. In his rage, Taranis did not see where he thrust his spear. He wounded even Ancasta, whom Tir held very tightly to himself.

Seeing at last that his spear was useless—by that time the blood of his bride and sons and hounds was running through the sky—he ordered Tir into his horse form and commanded him to forever carry his brother through the sky, making a dismal thunder as he went.

A thunderclap and a gust of rain-streaked wind cut the song short. Dser jerked his head around toward the doorway and everyone sat up very still like rabbits. Indi felt his heart in his throat.

The white-cloaked figure of the priest stood in the doorway. It held a staff of oak in its right hand. The other hand was flung upward a moment later, and an eerie, terrible voice shrieked, "*Tir!* Tir will have revenge!"

Indi got to his feet somehow, vaguely aware of others standing around him, his eyes fixed on the crazed holy man. He expected every moment for the thunder to distil into a stallion's tail of lightning and fire the roof beam over his head.

"*Tir!*" the priest screamed on. "Taranis will not ride Tir much longer! Tir will have his revenge! Revenge! *Revenge!*"

No one dared silence him. Quickly, a clear ring was thrust out from the wind-lashed priest. The dogs, Thern among them, howled wildly, and Indi felt his hair stand on end.

There was a lightning flash, and the priest's voice stopped. His form was dark against the sheer white backdrop, and when the light passed, the doorway was empty.

There was a tense, sizzling atmosphere in the hall afterward. Indi felt as though he had just retched up his heart, his belly empty and throbbing. Even Matheorex the Chief at the far end of the hall on his dais was silent and grim-faced. "It seems," he said softly, speaking through the heavy silence, "that if Taranis will overlook the song, Tir certainly will not."

Dser got to his feet and tucked his harp under his arm, his hand on his boy's shoulder. "It was Tir's song, my lord," he said calmly. Of all in the room, he seemed the most composed. "But perhaps I will not be singing it again for a while."

Matheorex nodded. "Perhaps, my friend, that is a wise thought." Then he raised his hand and, leaning forward, spoke to all his retainers. "Sit down and eat. Leave the wars of the gods to the gods and the priests. Perhaps they will leave us alone."

And somehow Indi found himself folding down onto the bench again. He found the food all in its place, his cup where he had left it. Odd—he had expected it to have all vanished away. He did not want to eat now. As the talk slowly returned to a boiling in the room and the priest's performance was slowly pushed aside, he sat quietly in his place, fingering his cup, thinking about his mother's dream. The thought of the brown voice seemed almost a relief. Better Tir and Taranis should forget their quarrel and fight some other battle, far from them. If only the wars of the gods would stay among the gods!

Cynr, noticing his friend's distraction, asked, "Has it put you so off your feed as that, Indi?"

The young man blinked into the present. He flushed unexpectedly, embarrassed that Cynr had caught him brooding over distant holy matters. If it were not for his mother's dreams, he might be as easy as the others now. "So? Perhaps it has," he replied noncommittally.

But Cynr cast him a sidewise glance and prodded, "If I did not know you better, I would say your conscience is uneasy."

Indi frowned back. "But you know me better," he said flatly. Then, by way of explanation, "It is that my mother has been dreaming of the gods."

"Truly? And what did the priest say?"

Indi looked round at the door, suddenly not liking its gaping emptiness at his back. "Would you like to come down to the Holy Place with me and ask?"

THE BROWN VOICE

HALF A MILE AWAY FROM the Chief's steading, deep into the woods, was the Holy Place. There was a low turf building with a stone doorway and the image of Tir carved in it, a huge, old oak tree growing in the centre of the clearing, and a heavy holiness surrounding the place. Indi and Cynr hardly dared go any farther in, but when they halted on the edge of the Holy Place, holding back their snarling hounds Thern and Moch-o, the priest stepped out of the building. Both men froze and their hounds stopped quarrelling.

Indi had never liked seeing the priest up close, and though there was a distance between them, it was too close for his liking at present. The old man's eyes burned bright in his wrinkled face; the old tattoo lines were faded and grey. He smelled eternally of blood but his robe was spotlessly white.

"The gods bless you, my sons," he said suddenly, showing none of his previous wildness. "I had been waiting for you."

Both Indi and Cynr were ready to back out, but still they did not dare. That they had come this far, or even thought of speaking with the mouthpiece of the gods, shocked them. Neither moved.

Angog the priest bowed. "It is your mother's dreams you wish to speak of, Indi map Matheorex? Why is Cynr with you?"

Indi recovered his tongue. "He wished to come along, lord, and I did not think to forbid it."

Cynr picked up his spear and planted his feet more firmly in place, determined not to leave Indi.

Angog shook his hands. "No, come here. The dreams are not meant for a woman but for a man to hear. Spoiled crops and slain babes are not in Tir's mind."

Indi gripped his spear with a white hand. If the customary calamities were not on the god's mind, what could be? Drought, starvation, plague—these were close enemies to Indi. What other thing could be lurking in the dark and holy future for his people?

Angog beckoned to them, pulling them forward with his eyes. Thern and Moch-co stayed on the edges of the wood, pacing back and forth, growling low in their throats. Indi's own hackles were up. He went round to the far side of the white ring that bounded the oak tree and waited with Cynr for Angog to speak. The priest stood facing them on the other side of the tree—the tree was forked low so they could gaze between the boughs—and held up his hands, palms to the sky, and shut his eyes. He began the sacred song of Tir, a song neither warrior understood. It made the young men feel even more tense and oppressed. It was worse than the thunderstorm.

At last Angog was done chanting, and he lowered his arms to his sides. In a strange, dead-level voice, he told them, "Tir has not planned rainless springs and failed crops. There is something worse coming upon us, something small and strong, something dark. It is the hand of Taranis, his spy; he must be found, or Tir will unleash his anger upon us. And there will be one among us who will follow the hand of Taranis and one who will die. Tir warns: he will have his revenge."

In the silence afterward, Indi counted his heartbeats slowly, one after another. It was the only thing to tell him he was still alive. The oppressive air of the clearing clouded his senses, and his heartbeat filled his ears with a low war drum sound.

"Thank you," he heard himself saying at last. "The gods have surely spoken; may they be heeded." He turned and rejoined Thern under the wood-eaves, Cynr at his tail.

Angog had only one more thing to say. "The thunderstorm was gentle last night; it will grow worse as time passes."

When the two men were out of the clearing and into the woods, they broke into a lope. Neither spoke. Their dogs ran beside them as they had been taught to do, leaping silently through the dense oak-scrub until they reached the open hill lands of the Downs. They came out of the last ragged stands of trees into the blistering pale open, and Indi stopped to suck in great lungfuls of air.

"That was a foolish, foolish whim of mine," he said, shaking himself like a dog to get the last feelings of holiness off. "I should never have gone."

Cynr laid his hand on his shoulder. "I am glad I went with you. Imagine facing that holiness alone...."

Indi shuddered. "I would rather not. Let us go see Cisha and her foal."

They walked up the narrow chalk track through the hot, clouded summer day. They were both naked to the waist and were sweating by the time they topped the highest hill and stood looking down on the Horse Valley. The dun lay over the hill at their back to the east, and Matheorex's herd ranged in the valley before them. The pale track wound down before them and up the hill again, snaking toward the east one way and climbing up toward the distant city of Venta on the other, from which the traders came. Harebell and heather covered the fields, giving them a blue and purple hue. Because of the low-hanging clouds, the colours were blurred and dimmed considerably. The track was grey now, not white, and would soon be speckled when the rains came back.

After standing a moment on the crest of the hill, Indi and Cynr went down through the heather and harebell to the valley.

The herd of mares little heeded their approach, but when Indi lifted his whistle—muffled by the heavy air—and broke the silence, a red mare trotted out of the press, a little spindly shadow of a foal under her belly.

Indi took her questing muzzle in his broad hands and blew into her nostrils. A rough chuckle rumbled in his throat as the mare snorted and pricked her little ears. "She is a fine mare, isn't she?"

Cynr looked up from the black colt. "She is, but Indi, you promised me the colt, did you not?"

Indi nodded. "I did say I would give the black colt to my favourite brother. Yes, you may have him."

The two men clasped their arms about each other's shoulders and watched the mare and foal melt back into the herd. A dull wind stirred their loose scarlet cloaks and swept across their damp chests. Indi took in a deep breath. The feeling that had crept upon him from the Holy Place, of darkness and foreboding, had not left, not after the run and the horses, not even with Cynr's reassuring presence. *Am I being every kind of fool?* he wondered, narrowing his eyes against the flat silver light of the overcast day. *Why can I not shake it off?*

Moch-co jumped up suddenly and Thern stiffened beside him, letting out a mournful growl. Indi stiffened as well, for it was the half longing, half hating growl of a dog to the wolf kind. He swung, his spear loose, and faced the western end of the valley. "Hist!" he whispered. "Cynr, look!"

Downwind, loping slowly and creeping like Tir's clouds, was a big black wolf. It was alone, which was odd, but it was so huge that Indi was not surprised. Its golden eyes surveyed the herd as it paced back and forth. The big cupped ears pricked as it heard Thern's challenge and welcome, and seeing the two humans, it sat down on its big haunches, gazing steadfastly.

Indi licked his lips and took a firmer hold on the enamelled shaft of his spear. It was a great spear, the spear of a chieftain's son. Cynr was doing the same with his own plain hunting spear, licking his lips and gripping the weapon tightly. A wolf was a fell thing to meet and kill. Both young men had done so, and they carried the scars to prove it.

"He means to kill one of the mares," Indi whispered. "We must kill him first."

"Take you Thern westward up the hillside and I will take Moch-co and cut the distance between him and the—"

A shrill whinny startled them. The wind had changed and the mares could smell the intruder. Bandr, the black colt, had gone into a wild frenzy and was running madly about. Cisha was trying to herd him back toward the east away from the wolf, but her attempts were foiled by the sudden thunderclap overhead and the rapid charge of the black wolf. Lightning streaked far off.

Thern howled the hunting call as Indi let go of his collar. Together they were running like stags across the valley floor, trying to help the mare before the wolf could get to either horse. The sky was very dark, and large, slow drops of rain were beginning to fall.

Indi had his spear couched and pulled back, ready to strike as he ran. Thern was a flash of brindle ahead of him, the wolf a blur of sable against the grey ground. Cisha was rearing, the black thing snapping at her breast as she lashed out at it. Bandr was being herded by Moch-co, but the colt was so terrified and disoriented, his noble efforts were useless.

Exactly when Indi joined the fray was so vivid it hurt to remember afterward. He remembered just clearing a hole in the ground and thinking a horse might break a leg in it, and he remembered ducking under Cisha's hooves, crashing headlong into the chest of the wolf. Thern and wolf mingled a moment then

Indi tasted blood. It was mixed with fur and a howl. Pain ripped against his breast, and claws scrambled at his thigh. The mare was screaming and galloping away, but she seemed to be Tir himself, galloping on top of Indi and the wolf. Was it Karmer—he wondered with a flash of terror—that he struggled with? Karmer the black Wolf? But no, gods did not bleed, no matter what the stories said. There was a flurry of black, the too-close shine of fangs in his face, and a grinding feeling shuddering up his spear as he dug into the animal's ribcage. He went over with the momentum of the body, crashing head over heels under the twitching wolf.

There was a blur of noises overhead, muffled by the raging throb of pain in his ears. He was bleeding: he could feel the wound gaping open and the blood warm and wet on his skin. Someone wrenched his spear out of his hand. Indi yelled a war cry in response, but the foreign hands pinned him down. Then the roaring pain overtook him and he was lost in the realms of the dead. After that, he was slowly aware of more pain, sharp, infrequent pain, the taste of mare's milk with heather-honey, and a myriad of voices.

One of them was brown.

The Beaded Sword

INDI WAS FIRST CLEARLY AWARE of the drum of rain over his head. Because of the pain in his head, he wished it would stop. The sound pounded in his brain, making his whole jaw ache as if it would fall off. His eyes were too heavy to open much, but he did catch the faintest glimmer of firelight through a crack in his eyelids. He kept his eyes shut and did not try to open them anymore; that one unsuccessful attempt had only made the thunder in his head increase. He was thirsty, and there was a lot of saliva in his mouth, but he was too sick with pain to swallow; the saliva pooled on his tongue and the side of his lips in an undignified manner. He hated the saliva and the rain. They were nuisances that he could not be rid of. He only wished to go back to sleep and sleep away the Tir wrath in his head.

When he awoke again, his headache was diminished and he was first aware of voices. The first he recognized as Angog's and he thought, *Is there a death in the house that he should be here? Is my father well?* But from the priest's words, it did not seem that either of these things were the case. Indi had a hard time sorting out what the priest had to say.

"He must go and he must go at once. Tir will kill this house with a smash of his hoof so terrible all the earth will feel it. The god of cloud and thunder is displeased. He has sent Karmer to inflict pain upon this house already, not a moment before this heretic came. And what say you? He has healed the boy? He is a friend of Taranis, the sworn enemy of Tir! Are you not horse-people, breeders and trainers of horses? Do you not owe your lives to the horse goddess Epona and the overlordship of Tir? Is this what you say? I tell you truly, he will not stand for this, not in his own house. He will have his revenge, great Chief. He will! He will!"

There was a long silence in which Indi frowned through his sleepiness and tried to untangle the priest's words. Then he heard the familiar rumble of his father, "Angog almighty, mouthpiece of the awful gods, I hear you well. But surely it is against the laws of our people—the horse-people—to turn out a stranger in the wilds of summer. And the services he has already performed for my household ... I cannot, with dignity, turn him away."

Once more there was silence. It was much longer than the one previous, and it occurred to Indi that this was a bad thing. Silence was a sign of intense anger and displeasure in priests. What was his father doing to upset Angog so?

At last Angog spoke. "Then, Chief Matheorex, you will keep the hand of Taranis here within your dun, before the very threshold of Tir's Holy Place?"

"If you put it so, Angog, I will."

The feel of dark holiness grew as Angog moved toward the door. "Very well, the laws of men will reign within the house of men, but in the houses of the gods it is a different matter. There it is different."

"I know that, worthy priest," Matheorex assured him softly. "Here within the dun I am lord and my word is law. Within the Holy Place, you are lord, and your word is law. So it is, so it shall be."

"So it is, but so it shall not always be," Angog replied. Then his presence departed and Indi felt the weight of holiness leave. He found he could breathe again, though it hurt terribly across his chest as the prick of the tattoos had hurt. For a moment he thought he was a boy again, lying on the pyre in the darkness, seeing Angog's hideous form etched against the bonfire. But then he was aware of the dream voice, the brown voice, speaking gently.

"You are king, lord Chief, but I hardly wish to stir up trouble in your dun."

"Nonsense, stranger, I will not turn you loose like a bad dog or a worthless mare. If you are the hand of Taranis, I will surely not anger him."

The voice came nearer to Indi. "I am not the hand of Taranis, great Chief, nor have I anything to do with him. Neither do I live under the white carving of Tir."

Indi began to feel hands on him, soft, kind hands with wrinkles in them. As a dog or a horse might, he sensed at once that the owner of the hands was friendly, but knowing it was a stranger he was a mite distrustful and pulled back his lips in a groggy snarl.

The brown voice laughed. "He is awake, the cubling is! Hush, do not bite these old hands, child. Let me tend your wounds."

"I am neither cubling nor child," Indi objected over his heavy tongue. "Where has Karmer gone?"

Matheorex came to his son's side and laid his hand on his forehead. "Maybe it was Karmer, maybe it was only the strange black wolf that is seen from time to time, alone, an outcast. Whoever it was, it got away with many wounds—more than you have—and will probably die. Cynr has gone after it. He left as soon as they brought you in, not content to rest until the wolf was caught. But you did well, my son."

Indi grinned at the compliment. Now he tried opening his eyes and found that he could see. To be sure, the world was blurry, but he could see the huge outline of his father and the smaller, less significant outline of the stranger. He was brown.

"Tirna Mother!" Indi cried, pulling away. "Are we all to die?"

The man in brown hushed him. "Of course, child," he said gently. "We all die sooner or later. Lie still or you will undo my good work."

Indi lay still and watched the stranger warily. He could remember quite clearly through the haze Angog's words about the stranger heretic, about the divine conspiracy that was coming upon them. His breath was coming quickly, for the wars of the gods were not something a man should see, and woe to the man caught up in them! He thought the hoof of Tir would at any moment come slicing through the roof beam of the houseplace and strike both brown man and himself dead. But nothing of the sort happened. Perhaps, Indi thought after a while, Angog had not yet told Tir about the brown man. Comforted by that thought, he looked the man over to see what sort of person he was.

The man was small, as Indi had first seen, but built to last, like a pony. He had short-cropped brown hair the colour of driftwood, black, glittering eyes with wings of laughter around them, a sharp, eagle-prow for a nose, a long brown robe, and a curious object hanging on a chain about his neck. Looking closer, Indi saw it was a little replica of a sword, so small it would fit easily into Indi's palm. It was made of shining red and gold beads, and Indi thought he had never seen anything more beautiful.

The bright eyes saw Indi looking at the sword. "Ah, you see the cross, child?"

Indi frowned. The man's tongue had trouble getting around his language, and here was a word totally foreign to Indi. "Forgive me," he mumbled.

"My cross," the brown man said, holding it out. Indi shrank from it. "No need to be afraid; it will not hurt you. It is only beads and thread, nothing more. It is the mark I live under, as your people live under the mark of Tir on the lintel."

"The beaded sword is the sign of your god?" Indi asked. "What sort of god have you?"

The brown man smiled kindly. "It would take a long time to answer that question, child. Let me finish mending you. Then, when we have leisure, I will answer that one for you."

Indi was silent for a while and let the brown man wash his wounds in his chest and thigh. The rain continued to drum overhead, the thunder to rumble far off. But presently he had to ask, "What does the beaded sword do for you, brown stranger?"

The man looked puzzled. "It does nothing for me, child. It is a sign, not a power. It shows who I am. That is all."

"What use is it, then?" Indi demanded. "If it does nothing for you—brings no protection, no good health, nothing—why wear it?"

"Because," the man replied levelly, "my God is my protection, my health, and my everything—and the beaded sword is proof of this. I will tell you of the beaded sword in time; you must be patient."

Indi fell silent once more, his head spinning. He shut his eyes and listened to the drum of rain outside. It would stop raining, but would the whirl of his brain stop? Indi knew without a doubt that this brown stranger was a holy man, but he also felt he was not a holy man as Angog was. He was not darkly holy and confusing like the dim, twisted barrows that Angog visited. Indi wanted to know more about this bright-eyed holy man who did not serve under Tir or Taranis. There was a powerful gentleness about the brown stranger, and as Indi watched through his sleepiness, he felt a glow within the man's hands and face. He liked the look of the beaded sword and wanted to know more about it. He feared Tir's wrath, but he hoped that he would get away with this curiosity for once, just once. Maybe Tir would not get angry. Maybe....

THE GOD OF THE WOODEN SWORD

IT TOOK A LONG TIME for Indi's leg to heal properly. The wolf had torn the inside of his leg, and much blood had been lost. The brown stranger laboured night and day without rest to keep Indi alive. First the fever had come, then the delirium, then a stretch of welcome darkness wherein Indi slept to healing. Thern lay beneath him, filling the silence with his worried whines. He knew his master was ill, but there was nothing he could do. He would not eat, and any hand that came near, save for the wrinkled, leathery hand of the brown stranger, he would snap at. Indi saw Cynr's face sometimes, his father's, and at times his sister's, but he could not reach any of them. He had dreams about the fine little beaded sword on the chain about the brown man's neck, and it seemed the only bright thing in his dark driftings.

A moon after the wolf attack in the Horse Valley, Indi was able to sit up and gaze about him. The serious summer storms had passed, and now the hot sun poured down through the smoke-hole in the roof and splashed over the threshold of the house-place. Thern joined the puppies in the sunlight, kicking them aside into tumbling rolls of fat and fur, to sit undisputed lord over the threshold. Indi watched him absentmindedly, groaning a little as he did so.

Lenag moved gracefully from the fire. "My brother, are you awake?" she asked softly.

Indi looked up, trying through his weak eyes to see her face. "Maybe I am," he muttered, "and maybe I still dream."

"Are you hungry?" she asked, taking him to be awake.

Indi put his hand over his belly, which felt so empty it hurt. "Yes, I am hungry. Give me what boils in yonder pot, sister; it smells of the gods' food."

Lenag took a red Samian bowl that was slightly chipped and very old, its slip all but worn away, poured some stew into it, and handed it to her older brother. "Let you eat, my brother. You will need your strength."

As she returned to her side of the fire, Indi ate and asked his questions. What had happened since he had been brought in from the fields with his leg all torn open? Who was the brown stranger? What dialogue had there been between the dun Chieftain and the priest of Tir?

Lenag took up her sewing as she replied to each question. "The black wolf got away, but Cynr went after it the same day you were brought in—your leg being all torn open—and cornered the wolf in a pine glen several leagues away. He felled it, but when he brought it back to skin it and make for you a winter's cloak, Angog took the skin from him in a blaze of prophecy. I was not told—the womenkind are never told, are they?—but it is my belief that Angog burnt the wolf for Tir's sake. It is in keeping with a foreign tale, a Red-Crest tale, he said, that when a god is burned, from its own ashes it rises again."

"We are *not* a Red-Crest people," interjected Indi hotly.

"Concerning the brown stranger," Lenag went on without looking up, "we little know anything of him. He speaks such strange things, brother!" Here she gave him a quick, confused glance. "He says nothing of Tir or Taranis or of the gods of other tribes—even the Red-Crests'—but he speaks of another God, one none of us have ever heard of. Christos, he is called, and he comes in the form of a man like us."

Indi stopped, his hand partway to his mouth. The stew dribbled back through his fingers into the bowl and onto the floor; a puppy came sniffing over to see if it was good to eat. "A man like us?" Indi finally asked, incredulous. "What sort of God is that? Do they not live in thunder and darkness and hide their ways from us?"

Lenag jerked her spool of yarn, not raising her eyes. "I am a woman, Indi. How should I know of the gods' ways?"

Indi was muttering to himself. "What sort of God ... surely it is the same God who has the brown stranger wear that curious sword about his neck! But he said he takes no power from it. How strange! Doesn't Angog take his power from the gods through the bones of animals and the phases of the moon?"

"Brother," Lenag said with a sigh, "I do not know. It is in my mind—but you are a Chieftain's son, who does not listen to women—that Angog's way is silly. Do the gods have to channel their powers through bones and moons? It is in my mind that this brown stranger gets his power directly from his God. Bones and moons, I think, are meaningless to him. His God would scoff at them."

Indi's eyes shot to the doorway. "Hush, Lenag," he said harshly. "What if someone should hear you?" He glanced at the carving of Tir.

Lenag looked up, startled at what she had said. "I am only a woman," she amended. "The gods will little take notice of me."

Indi thought for a moment that she was right and that the gods would overlook her runaway tongue. But not long after she and he had glanced back down at the things that occupied them, a dark shadow entered the room. Both heads flew up, eyes wide.

But it was only the brown stranger who stood in the doorway, his hand on Thern's head. The dog beat his tail and whined softly, thrusting his muzzle into the old, leathery hand. A little wind sighed around him, stirring the odd brown robe that he always wore, but not his hair, which was cropped close and made his head look like a furry egg.

"Ah, you rise, my son," the brown man said. He pushed past Thern and came into the houseplace. Lenag rose and bowed to him before returning to her work. Sitag, her younger sister, scrabbled hound-like in the shadows, yelping like a pup. The brown man gave her a little smile then moved to Indi's side. "How do you feel?" he asked, laying one cool hand on his bare shoulder.

Indi said nothing about the man's rough ways with his language; he forgave him that and the clear scent of Latin that fringed each word he spoke. "I feel stiff, sir, but otherwise whole and eager to be out on the hunting trail once more."

The man nodded. "Soon you shall be out. You have eaten?"

"Yes, I have eaten."

The brown man turned to Lenag. "Then suffer me to eat as well, for my belly hardly remembers the morning meal."

Lenag rose and got Indi's bowl, filled it, and handed it to the brown man. He smiled at her and said, "The Lord bless you, child."

Indi said nothing out of politeness as the brown man ate. He watched out of the corner of his eye as he gently spooned the stew with his cupped hands and ate it without a sound. When all was finished, Indi concluded that the man must have come from a great southern tribe over the water, for his manners were exquisite, and though he did not speak Indi's language with ease, he was well versed in Indi's ways.

The brown man beckoned to Indi. "Come, my son; let us walk together in the sunshine and strengthen your pent-up limbs."

Indi got to his feet. He was ashamed to find that his legs had gone all wobbly like a newborn pup's from his long stay in bed. But he made no mention of it, and he was glad that the brown man did not either but walked silently by Indi's side until they were out on the porch amid the hot sunlight and grey, fuzzy hound cubs. Indi breathed deep, lifting his nose to the bright, clear sky. A soft, warm wind was just stirring so that he could see the parched grass move but not feel it. A crow circled high in the air above him. Across the Downs hills, Indi could see the spread of the herd, dark and light against the green. He forgot the ache of his untried legs and wished to be off at once, running through the bending grass with the wild horse, leaping the crests of the hills, laughing at the startled neigh of a mare nearby. He longed to be away with Cynr on the river, diving naked into the silver stream, grasping the wild summer fish with his bare hands and wrestling them to shore.

The brown man broke the silence. "You wished to know about my cross, Chieftain's son?"

Indi jerked his head down to look at the little man. "Yes, I did wish to, if it is not too much to ask after."

"Certainly not," the brown man shook his head in a friendly way. "That is what I'm here for." He coughed as if he were beginning a long, important tale.

"My name, Indi map Matheorex, is Procyon. As you might be able to tell from my accent, I am from Gaul and was raised in the Latin way. My father was an old officer in the Sixteenth Gallica before he got his wound and his wooden foil. My mother, actually, was one of the Brigantes."

Indi raised a brow. "Indeed, is that true? You hardly look it."

Procyon smiled then chuckled briefly. "True, I don't look it. I was, as I said before, raised a good Gaulish Roman. I might have gone into the military like my father did, but I went into the church instead."

Indi wanted to ask what that might be and what it entailed, but he restrained himself. He should not have spoken out about Procyon's ethnicity.

"I don't suppose any of my kind have ever come here before," Procyon went on thoughtfully, looking round him a trifle bewilderedly. "That is why I came. You see, the church's work is to spread the word of God throughout the world, and here am I, little brown Procyon in Britannia, doing just that."

Indi looked at him oddly. There was a pause, and Procyon seemed to have finished speaking. "What God?" Indi asked at length.

"The only God," Procyon replied without batting an eyelid. "The God of my beaded sword."

Indi's fair brows shifted downward. "Your God that gave you the beaded sword, eh? Tell me—is he like Taranis? Does he ride the summer storms?"

Procyon shook his head. "Certainly not. The Lord is in His holy temple; the Lord's throne is in heaven."

"What? Do not all the gods dwell in heaven?" Indi asked hotly, spreading his hands out and upward. The brown man was kind, but he did not understand the gods. They might overlook Lenag's talk but not a man's. No, certainly not a man's; a man should know better. "Of course they do," Indi went on, digging his bare toe angrily into the dust. "Everyone knows that. Oughtn't you be careful?"

Procyon was not angry in the least. He crooked an old, well-used but genuine smile, and replied, "I said to the Lord, 'You are my Lord; I have no good besides You.' The sorrows of those who have bartered for another God will be multiplied; I shall not pour out their drink offerings of blood, nor will I take their names upon my lips."

Indi stared at Procyon. He stepped back gingerly, fully expecting a bolt from Tir to fly from the sky and strike the brown man down. When nothing happened, Indi remembered Procyon's words of earlier when he had been sick: *"I am not the hand of Taranis, great Chief, nor have I anything to do with him. Neither do I live under the white carving of Tir."* He remembered the glow in his hands and face and the holy-man feeling that emanated from him. Indi felt his hackles lift on the nape of his neck.

"Far be it from me to deny a god," Indi hesitated. "But how is he different from Taranis and Tir? How is he different from the Red-Crests' gods, or the gods of anyone? Are they not all the same with different names?"

Procyon sat down wearily on a timber. He was old, Indi saw, and his limbs needed rest. "Oh, my dear son, that is certainly a point of conjecture. I have not been told whether or not the creatures you call gods are only a few with many names or lots of different beings. But that is hardly the question."

"I should rather think," replied Indi, once more growing hot and indignant, "that it *is* the question."

"Certainly you would think that," Procyon responded levelly. He was hardly ruffled by Indi's flashing glare and his fists. Indi was put out at the brown man's calm demeanour and the way he was unable to disturb him. "Most certainly, because those creatures are all you have known. I was just so once. Mithras, Jove, Thor—I worshiped a score of gods once. But then I was brought to the realization that these gods—each and every one of them—are totally false."

"Holy Tir!" Indi cried, retreating further. "You shall kill us all!"

Procyon shook his head. "No, I shan't. Your gods have absolutely no hold over me, but they do hold sway over you and your people."

Indi crooked a brow. "They hold sway, eh, those who are false?"

"You would hardly call a man a friend if he played you wrong, would you?" the brown man replied calmly. "Of course they are false; they lead you away from the truth and blind your eyes—as they are trying to do now—and they claim your soul as their own. But they're not real gods, Indi map Matheorex, they only pretend to be. They're traitors, trying to be the one true God. That's why they're false. They hide themselves in shadow and darkness, torment your minds with dark spells, and whisper witches' sweet words to you. They are false."

Indi crouched down on the balls of his feet, trying to look calm. He glanced at the clear sky and felt a dark oppression in his soul. "You make them sound so evil and malicious, holy man from afar," he said slowly. "How would you know?"

Procyon nodded. "I make them sound that way because they *are* that way. And if the gods—as you call them—are only a few with many names, then serving as a slave under Mithras and Jove and Thor, I learned what they are like. They are not like my true God, my God of—of the wooden sword."

Indi gritted his teeth in frustration. "So, are you saying there is only one real God?"

"There can be only one real Chieftain in a dun, can't there?" Procyon asked back.

Seeing he would get no satisfactory answer there, Indi tried again. "Lenag my sister said that your God was called Christos and that he was a human. Only the Red-Crests worship humans. Are you just a Red-Crest in brown?"

Procyon shook his head. "I am not a Red-Crest. But yes, your sister heard rightly. His name is Christos in the Greek language—but you do not know that tongue. It is also Jesus; Jesus Christos."

"It means all of naught to me," Indi shrugged.

"Jesus means *salvation* in its old tongue. Christos is the Greek form of *Messiah* in the old tongue, which was the redemption of God's chosen people."

Indi laid his arms across his knees and stared levelly at Procyon. Was he completely out of his mind? "Gods or one God, they are not the sort to touch us in kindness," Indi said stoutly. "Do you know nothing of Angog the priest? Tir will hardly speak to him, let alone us, and whenever he does speak it is of dark things."

"Because Tir is evil," said Procyon. "What else would there be? But not my God. My God is holy."

"As are all the gods," Indi insisted. "Why else would they be gods?"

"No," replied the brown man, "they only come in a form that they tell you is holiness. None of us could really look upon holiness, Indi. It is too much for our eyes to handle."

"So." Indi accepted that for the sake of argument. "What use is that? How can your God save or redeem His—His whatever you called them—the 'chosen people'?"

Procyon held up a hand for a moment of patience and settled himself more comfortably on the timber. "That is where the wooden sword comes in. You see, Indi, my God is a kind God. He is holy, righteous, and just, loving, gracious, a Father to His people. Long, long ago—"

"Ho!" Indi cried. "This is a story?"

"Yes," Procyon replied, his eyes showing something near ruffled but not quite. "Long, long ago, before the Red-Crests ever lived, before your people ever lived, across miles and leagues of sea and land, at the very beginning of time, there were two people made by God, made good: a man and a woman."

"Let me guess," Indi said, smiling. "The man stole the woman from your God, your God grew angry and banished the man, the man came back and—"

"Indi, I told you before that my God is not like your gods in any way. No, the man was made first from the dust of the ground, and God breathed life into him. The man tended the earth, for it was his pleasant task, but from among the animals and earth he could find none fit to be his helper. So God made Adam, the man, fall into a deep sleep."

"I can't say I'm liking this story," Indi frowned warily, rocking back on his feet. "What did your God do next?"

"A perfectly fine thing," Procyon assured him. "He took from Adam's side part of his flesh, and from that he made a woman. Adam awoke, saw that she was perfect for him, and named her Eve."

Indi ran the two names over his tongue. "Strange names."

"They are in their language," Procyon explained. "But to the point, there were only those two humans in all the world, and all the world was perfect. There was no war, no sickness, no famine."

"None of those things that Tir will bring upon us because of you," Indi sighed. "Continue."

"God placed Adam and his wife in a beautiful garden and told them to tend it faithfully," continued Procyon. "But there was one condition: in the centre of the garden there was a tree, the tree of the knowledge of good and evil, and they were not to eat of that tree. Of any other tree, most certainly they could eat, but not that tree. If they did, they would die."

"Why not?" Indi demanded. "What was wrong with that tree? You said everything was perfect."

Procyon rubbed his chin. "I think, my son, that it was an occasion to serve God in faithfulness by obeying his command. God's children do not always know the *why* of what He says, but that should not stop us from obeying him. When you are young, your father tells you not to run in front of the mares. Why? you ask. What is wrong with that? You're too young to know, but he knows."

"All the same," Indi replied, "I should find it awfully hard not to take a bite of the fruit. Was it good?"

"Yes, as you will hear in a moment. Here we have to return to your gods. Once—when exactly we humans don't know—there was a noble creature that served God diligently. He was the greatest of the angels, which God made. What they are like is hard to say, since we humans practically never see them. But he got it into his head that he would be equal to—no, greater than—God Himself."

"So, here is where your God banishes someone in anger, and then this angel comes back eventually and trumps your God."

"Patience, Indi!" Procyon sighed. "You get ahead of me, and you've not quite got it right. Of course he came back, but he didn't trump God. Oh no, he tried, and God turned and slammed him into the ground as if he were no more than a fly. He's not dead yet, but his time is running short."

Thern rose from his crouch and barked once in greeting. Indi and Procyon looked round to see Cynr coming up the timber steps toward them, Moch-co jumping at his heels. Indi felt relieved to see his friend and a little embarrassed to be with the heretic holy man.

"You are up and out," said Cynr, coming to a halt beside him. It was the obvious thing to say and awkwardly said, but Indi saw Cynr was glad to see him. "How is it?"

"It aches," Indi replied honestly. "It aches, but far better it ache out here in the sun than in that stuffy room."

Cynr jerked a smile across his face and swung round, addressing Procyon out of courtesy. "A good day to you, old father."

Procyon tucked a little smile of his own at the corner of his mouth. "A good day to you, my son. And good day to you—" he stretched out his hand and ruffled the fur behind Moch-co's ears. "A good dog," he said, looking up.

Cynr twisted his mouth wryly. "A good dog," he said, and was quiet.

Feeling awkward for the two of them, for they seemed to be a little strained between each other, Indi interjected by way of explanation, "Procyon has been telling me the story of his deity."

"Has he?" Cynr squatted down and pulled Moch-co's ears through his fingers. "And has it been a good tale in the telling?"

Indi could not answer that, not knowing himself if it was a good tale, knowing only that it was leaving him with the taste of thunder in his mouth. The brown man waved one hand dismissively. "The story is written by the one it is about, and the writer is good. But you have made me lose my thoughts. Where was I?"

"The angel," Indi prompted. He was aware of Cynr settling himself more firmly beside him.

"Ah, yes. Now, the angel, or the serpent, as he is called, was the most subtle and sweet of all God's creatures. He met the woman in the garden and—"

"Well, he *would*, wouldn't he?" growled Indi presumptuously.

Procyon gave him a stern look. "No, he didn't. The serpent asked her, 'Has God said that you can eat of every fruit of every tree in the garden?' And she said, 'From every tree, yes, but not from the tree that is in the middle of the garden. He has said, "In the day that you eat of the fruit of that tree you will surely die."' But the serpent said, 'You will not surely die! God knows that when you eat the fruit of that tree your eyes will be opened. You will be like God, knowing both good and evil.'"

Indi leaned forward, caught up in spite of himself in a good, unheard story. "But that's what the angel wanted for himself. Why was he going to make the woman do it?"

"Because," Procyon said, "the angel knew that their fate would be like his if they tried. And he hated the humans because they were God's most treasured creation, so he purposed to do what mischief and damage to them as he could."

"What happened?"

"The woman looked at the fruit and saw it was beautiful and desirable to make one wise. So she took the fruit and ate it."

"Just like a woman," Cynr said mildly.

"And," Procyon continued, "she gave some to her husband and he ate, too."

Cynr looked up through the dark forelock of his hair, frowning. "Him too? Desirable to make one wise indeed."

Procyon sighed, as if the fate of the two grieved him deeply. "Well, the serpent was right: it opened their eyes. Before then all had been perfect, but now they realized that they were naked, and they were ashamed. So they made coverings for themselves from plants."

"If they were the only humans," Indi objected, "and husband and wife, what difference did it make?"

Procyon only looked at him long and hard, and Indi was content with the answer he read in his eyes.

"After that," Procyon continued aloud, "the two heard the sound of the Lord walking through the garden in the cool of the day. Because they had disobeyed Him—and trust me, it is a terrible thing to face the holy God when you have disobeyed Him—they were afraid and hid themselves. The Lord called for Adam, and of course Adam had to answer. 'I heard the sound of You walking in the garden,' he said, 'and I was afraid because I was naked, so I hid.' The Lord said, 'Who told you that you were naked? Have you eaten of the tree I forbade you to eat of?'"

"I'll warrant your God was furious," Indi smiled. "He shot them to bits with his fury like arrows, didn't he, and created a new people, the chosen ones, of whom you are certainly a part?"

"He was angry," Procyon replied, "but He knew all along that this was going to happen."

Indi frowned.

Procyon nodded. "My God knows everything, Indi. How else would He be anything other than *God*?"

Still in that mild tone, Cynr said, "Just like the gods; force men to rebel and then punish them for it."

"I have been reminding Indi many times," Procyon said very sternly, "that my God is *not* like your gods."

"Oh?" said Cynr. "If your God knew that his two humans would do this evil—if it was indeed an evil—why did He not stop them? They have disobeyed Him and they must be punished. He has allowed them to disobey Him, so where is the justice in their punishment? What makes your God's fury any different from the fury of my own?"

Indi looked up from rubbing at the ache that was still in his leg. He had not thought of it so, and for a moment it seemed true. But a moment later, looking into Procyon's suddenly fierce and shining face as the man warmed to the challenge, he knew the brown stranger could not love an unjust God. Heretic or not, Procyon could not love cruelty.

"That is a question within a question," said Procyon. "And you will not sit still long enough to hear it all out. Let it suffice to know that my God ordained all this because He had something even better planned. That's why Adam and Eve sinned. God made everything good in the beginning, but that was not enough for Him. He had planned something even better to come. My beaded sword."

Indi eyed the object once more. It glittered like embers in the clear, hot sunlight and flashed like the gold from over the Western Sea. "But you said that it had no powers, holy man," he replied hesitantly. His brain was in a whirl.

"No, my beaded sword does not, but the *wooden* sword—which this is fashioned after—signified a terrible power. You see, Indi—Cynr—when Adam failed to obey God, God did punish them: their bodies fell from immortality and slowly they died, just like all of us. The serpent was punished as well, of course. God is just. But in the beginning God made a promise to His people: out of woman would come a seed of redemption. The serpent would bruise him on the heel, but he would crush the serpent's head. His people would be won back from having sold themselves to the overlordship of evil."

"This is where the serpent tried to revenge himself upon your God, and your God crushed him?"

Procyon nodded. "The same. But it did not happen immediately. Thousands of years went by, but God had His faithful followers. In time I will tell you of them all. One of them was able to talk to God face to face—more or less—and when he came out from speaking with God, his face was shining from the seared glory of the Holy One, and all the people were afraid and bade the man to veil himself. No one can stand the glory of God."

Indi remembered the oppression of the Holy Place and how the scent of blood and burnt fur hung like a cloud over it, and the presence of Tir was unmistakable throughout. "What about this wooden sword?" he asked, brushing away the memory.

"The wooden sword is a Red-Crests' invention," continued Procyon. "They do not use it now—Emperor Constantine outlawed the brutish practice—but the memory remains. The wooden structures stood a foot or so higher than a man, and a criminal was nailed wrist and foot to the cross and body-pieces of the sword and hung there to die. He could not breathe without forcing himself up by his nailed feet, which was very painful, and in the end he would expire by suffocation."

"Gruesome and effective," said Cynr, his teeth showing as he spoke. "It would be a good deterrent from breaking the law."

Indi stared into the dust. He tried to picture the gruesome machine of death in his own mind. He recalled seeing an offender drowned in a marsh but never hung on wood. "Wrist and—foot?"

Procyon held out his hands and his sandaled feet. "Through here—and here—and here," he pointed, "with iron nails about so large. It is extremely painful, and the man does not die immediately."

"I do not understand the Red-Crests' ways," Indi said sourly. "I do not understand, and I do not wish to. Thank the gods they have gone from us at last."

"But that was what the serpent used to bruise the woman's seed," Procyon said. "The woman's seed was the Son of God."

"So it was not your God himself who hurt," Cynr smiled wryly. "How very like the gods."

"No," replied Procyon with amazing patience. "It was my God. He was born of a virgin through His Holy Spirit, which was a miracle long foretold, and He was both fully man and fully God."

Indi, who had been thinking like Cynr, shrugged. "Far be it from me to question what the gods do," he remarked dryly. "If he is both man and God, so be it."

In the paddock, a horse whinnied; the sound of it carried across the distance, echoing off the surrounding hillsides. It was a very lonesome, familiar sound.

"God had to become a man," Procyon explained. "Man had disobeyed God and therefore deserved to die, for God deserves—and demands—perfect obedience in all things. But man could never repay the debt he owed his God, so in His mercy God, being a perfect man—for sin could not touch Him—lived a perfect life and died, paying our debt for us."

"So your Christos is dead?" Indi asked. "Your God is dead? What good is a dead God?"

"He did not remain dead." That smile flashed again. "This is where the seed crushed the serpent's head. Death is the punishment for sin, and because the Christos was perfect and sin could not touch Him, He rose from the dead, alive, breaking the powers of death and the grave, and giving the promise of eternal life to His people, for He is indeed a very loving God."

There was a hot, muggy silence after that. Cynr gestured with one hand, as though that were that. Thern, who had been lying not far off, scratched at a beetle.

"And that was the end," Indi sighed. It was a better story than many he had heard.

"Oh no, it was only the beginning," laughed the brown man. "Before, the salvation of men belonged to only a small people, but since Christos rose again, it has expanded everywhere to all tribes. This was the great other thing God had planned; this was the wonder He had prepared to display His power and love. That is the reason I am here, to spread the news that now there is a hope."

"Hope?" Indi asked crossly. "Hope for what? We are not gods; we do not live forever. What hope?"

"The hope," Procyon answered, with an odd sort of smile on his face that told Indi he was very wrong, "that was given by the wooden sword."

The Archer's Cuff

Despite the dark looks from Angog the priest, Matheorex continued to house Procyon the monk from Oversea. And despite the dark looks from Angog the priest, Procyon the monk continued to preach his hope. Indi sat by him silently, listening to the stories of strange-named people. He enjoyed the stories; who of his people did not enjoy a new story? But the tales meant nothing to him. He refused to understand the meaning of sin as Procyon defined it. Christos was just another God among so many; what difference did it make if Indi served him or not? It was possible, he reasoned, that Procyon was mistaken and Christos was really just Taranis.

But deep inside Indi feared it was not so.

He got his wish to swim in the river with Cynr. Occasionally his leg would cramp so that he could hardly walk, but after a while the pains went away and he was able to run down the slopes to the woods, a cloak slung over his shoulder.

A bird's whistle broke the soft, summer air. Indi drew up, waited for it to come again, and replied to it. Then little dark Moch-co came wriggling out from under the bracken, and Cynr dropped from a tree branch.

"Ho!" he cried, a dark smile on his face. "You've got away from that brown-clad holy man, have you?"

Indi shrugged. "He is not a bad man, Cynr, and he does tell good stories."

"Perhaps he had better become a blind bard like Dser and stop his priesting," his friend replied. "At any rate, he is arrogant, and he makes my hackles stand so."

Nodding, Indi said, "So, he makes mine stand also. But Thern likes him—that is something."

"Thern likes any who will throw him a bone and say, 'Good pup!'" Cynr laughed. Then, sobering, he asked, "And the leg—did he at least mend that properly?"

Indi reddened. "He has mended it."

Cynr shrugged, reddening himself. "I—I rather wished it had been me—and not you—who spilled blood with the wolf that day."

Indi looked sidelong at his friend. His lips were tight-shut and his eyes were steadily facing forward. "Are you still sore about the black wolf pelt, then?" he inquired.

Cynr gave a harsh bark of laughter. "I had hardly time then to be sore about it, friend, when it was taken from me. But leagues of running here and there, crossing the path with Moch-co a thousand times before I finally cornered the brute … yes, I would be sore. But Tir wanted the pelt, and that is that."

Indi heard himself saying, as though to ease the ache for his friend a little, "Procyon does not think much of Tir …"

But Cynr suddenly flared, face darkening. "Tir wanted the pelt, and that is that. I do not care what Procyon thinks. Let us not talk of him anymore."

Indi backed off, and they talked about more pleasant things after that: Bandr would be broken in next springtime; Cisha had a sore foot but was mending; the three-year-olds had been broken and were waiting for the traders from Venta. But he could not quite brush off Cynr's sudden fury at Procyon, who was nice, even if he was a heretic.

At last the two young men reached the river. It was wide and deep and slow and mirrored the dark, green reflections of the trees overhead. Thern and Moch-co did not wait for their masters; they plunged to their tipped-up chins in the cool water, barking as they got water in their mouths.

Indi laughed; it felt good to laugh, and he stripped as quickly as he could. The red line of his wound still showed on his leg, but, testing the cat-gut strings the kept the lips of skin together, he found it would hold, and he plunged after his hound into the river. Cynr came after him, springing through the air. Water splashed on all sides the way snow flies from under a running horse's feet in winter.

Indi turned on his back and floated about the wide pool in the river. The water ran over him, tickling him like feathers. The blue sky was so bright overhead that he could hardly look at it. The leaves danced in a wind. Thern barked on the opposite bank. *Forget the wars of the gods,* Indi muttered in his mind as he turned over and dove for the stones at the bottom of the river. Coming up he concluded, *They are too much for a man.*

As the sun was beginning to redden in the western sky, Indi and Cynr climbed out of the delightful river and shook off with their hounds. They dried and dressed and made their way back to the dun. They walked slowly so as not to get too hot and ruin the good of their bath, but when they reached the open chalk track, they realized that something was going on at the dun. Thern and Moch-co, sensing excitement, ran yelping up the road before their masters.

"What could it be?" Cynr asked, standing still in the middle of the way. Both of them were gazing upward, their hands shielding their eyes against the still bright sun.

Indi moved forward. "I do not know. Come, let us see."

They ran together up the white path, dodging the loose milch cows that the little boys without their tattoos were herding. One shouted something to Indi, but Cynr called back hotly, "Don't talk to your Chieftain-son, little cur!"

Even with the sun going down there was hardly any wind, and there was none at all in the courtyard of the dun. Also there was such a crowd that what air there might have been was all but used up. Indi felt the staleness of the air slap him as he ran forward and slowed, pushing his rightful way through the press. Cynr trailed along behind him, peering over his shoulder.

There was a stranger standing near the timber steps with Chieftain Matheorex. His hair was long and black, and his eyes were sharp, almost cunning. But there was a clean hound-grin on his face. He was grinning at Tirna, who stood by her husband, a length of beautiful red-and-orange striped cloth in her arms. It was splayed out, billowing lightly as she moved it. One look at her face and Indi knew the trader would go away without the cloth and Tirna Chieftain-wife would have another dress presently.

But Matheorex, the freckles in his rough face standing out starkly in the late light, was not concerned with cloth for dresses. He was testing a pilum in his hand, his red brows crunched together in thought.

Indi moved to Procyon's side. He saw Cynr cast him a strange, dark look and move away a little, but Indi bent down to Procyon's ear. "Who is the trader, holy man?"

Procyon smiled his welcome to Indi. "A Spaniard, I think," he replied. "He has already sold a glass necklace to Lenag for the two counter-weights of a spear. Your father was displeased."

"Why should the Chieftain-daughters not be pretty?" Indi smiled. "What does he think of the cloth?"

Procyon's eyes glittered. "You know him better than I."

Indi's eyes glittered back. "Yes, he likes it. Under that scowl he likes it."

There was a moment of silence between the two. They listened carefully to the Spaniard and Matheorex talking.

"It is a Red-Crest weapon, lord," the trader from Venta explained. "It is used to throw into the shields of the enemy. The spear bends on impact so that it is hard to get out, making the shield useless or cumbersome."

Matheorex frowned deeper. "It bends, does it? What good is a war spear that bends? I have only two hands, and I shall need them for everything of worth. Nay, take back the Red-Crest weapon."

The trader shrugged and took the pilum back. Next he produced a slender ash-bow with a thin string. He plucked the string once, and a beautiful musical note leapt into the air. Thern's head went up under Indi's restraining hand. Procyon smiled slightly and watched with detached interest.

As the trader ran his hand along the bow, Matheorex watched him under his thick brows. Indi knew the trader was watching his father as well, but suddenly a voice spoke up, "The bow, is it for a chieftain only, or for others as well?"

It was Cynr who had spoken. He had moved back and stood leaning against the doorway of one of the huts, his arms folded across his chest. His head was tipped back a little to see over the crowd, but the bow had caught his eye. Indi smiled; Cynr had always liked the bow, ever since they had been cubs together.

At a gesture from the Chieftain, the trader held out the bow. Cynr pushed off the doorpost and strode closer. He stood leaning for a moment over the bow, his sharp eyes flicking up and down it expertly. He plucked the string gently, producing a softer, more elusive sound. The trader's eyes gleamed as he gazed at Cynr's face, but Cynr was not disturbed.

"It is beautiful," he said slowly, raising a brow. "What will you take for it?"

The trader's face was masked. "It is a rare bow, I can assure you. It comes from Egypt by way of the Red-Crests' road. There are few like it in Britannia."

"What will you take for it?" Cynr repeated firmly, his hand hovering inches from the bow.

"A good watch-dog," the trader replied, eying Moch-co at Cynr's heels. "It is an uncertain road to Portus Adurni, and the horses will need a good four-legged drover, I am thinking."

Cynr said, "I am thinking you drive a hard bargain."

But the trader merely turned his head and looked back out of one eye, as a bird will do.

Indi pricked his ears to see what Cynr would do. For one moment his friend's face clouded in uncertainty. Moch-co whined, as if he knew what was at stake.

At last Cynr dropped his hand from the bow. Indi breathed a sigh. But Cynr clasped his hound's collar and slipped it loose. "Take the hound, trader from afar," he said. "I will take the bow."

Indi was shocked. He looked hard at Cynr's face, trying to capture his eye, but his friend did not look up. He took the bow out of the trader's hand and shoved Moch-co at the trader. The hound whined shrilly, scrabbling after Cynr, but Cynr turned, looked at him sternly, and said, "Kah! You have a new master now. Bad dog! Hush your noise."

Moch-co lowered his ears and sank belly-to-earth where he sat. The trader sighed and patted the hound's head in a kind fashion, but Indi still thought him hard to drive such a bargain. The only consolation was that the trader would not ill use Moch-co.

The trader brought out another article that he flashed to catch Cynr's eye. It was a round stone archer's cuff, very beautiful and so smooth one could see one's face in it. Cynr raised a brow. "A cuff? What would you take for that?"

The trader gestured to the leathern strap in Cynr's hand. "Let me have the collar and you can have the cuff, so?"

"So." Cynr took the cuff and tied it onto his left wrist.

Indi was not aware of much else that happened. Beside him, Procyon seemed divided, looking after Cynr with obvious concern as the young man stalked away through the crowd. And when the trader gathered himself up and began down the uncertain road to Portus Adurni, Indi had to hold Thern back from running wild after Moch-co. He held him back, but he could not shut the dog's muzzle as he cried after his friend. The last of the three-year-old horses was a dark form on the chalk road as the sun went down; only a thin red line broke the horizon from the black above.

Moch-co's frantic cry echoed over the Downs.

Bride Fires Burning

Because Chieftain Matheorex refused to banish Procyon from the dun, Angog's presence was all but removed from society. He was now only a white-shrouded figure standing straight and tall afar off, glaring with jewel-bright eyes. Whenever Indi saw him his hackles shot sky high, but he dared not say anything for his conscience was uneasy. Every time he saw the priest he heard Procyon's words, the same words over and over, *"I am not the hand of Taranis, great Chief, nor have I anything to do with him. Neither do I live under the white carving of Tir,"* and he dreaded the revenge of the gods.

The crops were planted long ago and now the dun watched the growing with patient, anxious eyes. They petitioned Tir for a good harvest, but after those first tumultuous storms, the sky remained clear. A foal went lame and died out in the hills. Angog's eyes grew brighter still.

A few days after the departure of the Venta trader, Indi came out of the houseplace and found Procyon sitting on the doorsill, his chin in his hands. There was a long, sad expression on his face.

"What ails you, old father?" Indi asked, sitting down next to him.

Procyon bent his head toward an old woman who was facing her house, kissing her hands and placing them over the form of Tir on her doorway. She was muttering under her breath as she did so.

Indi looked back at Procyon. "She is asking Tir for a good crop. All the old ones do it."

Procyon shook his head. "I know, Indi. I tried to get her to stop, but she would not listen. All the world will not listen. Sometimes I think that there is not an ear made to hear anywhere." With a shaky sigh he put his head down in his hands. When he raised his head, there were tears on his face. Indi frowned; it was not acceptable to weep. But Procyon cried out, "Lord, why are their hearts so hard? Open their eyes to see Your mercy and their hearts to receive Your Spirit!"

Indi got up and left Procyon on the doorsill to cry out to his own God. He went down past the huts and walked aimlessly out onto the road. He thought of searching out Cynr, but for some reason the young man had been absent lately. Indi half wondered if it had to do with Moch-co leaving, but Cynr had gotten a fresh hound pup with plenty of potential. For all Indi could see, Moch-co was forgotten.

When Indi stood outside the walls of the dun, he gazed around him in some surprise. His feet had taken him rather blindly to where he stood, and now that he was aware of his surroundings, he did not know what to do with himself. The sky was clear and the ground hot; there was still no wind, and, looking down at the fields, Indi felt a quick pang of fear when he saw the crops tinged brown. He looked back at the sky and begged the gods for rain. But even as he did so, he knew—he knew well—that it was Tir's wrath against them that held off the rains.

"Clear sky."

Indi jumped and gripped his hunting spear. The smell of dark holiness caught him by the throat and made him gag, for beside him, walking up on silent, bare feet, was the priest Angog.

The young man saluted in haste and moved away, but the fierce eyes followed him. "You know it is your fault," Angog remarked. "If it were not for you—your life still living after Karmer attacked you—the rains would come."

Indi shuddered. "No, it was the brown man who healed me. He is a holy man, too. Obviously some God wishes me alive, else I would not be."

Angog glared at him until Indi had to drop his eyes. Shame washed over the young man's face when he thought he could stand against wolves and warriors but not a single priest. "The brown man is our enemy," Angog said sternly. "He comes from Taranis, and a suckling child could tell his words are the words of foolishness. A Red-Crest sword freeing men? Indi map Matheorex, are you so very young that you cannot see the foolishness of this?"

Indi did not let Angog get any further. For once Indi lost his head, flaring at the priest. "I am neither young nor foolish!" he cried hotly. He pointed a strong, tanned finger at Angog. "And let you remember that I am the son of the Chief."

"Let you remember," Angog called as Indi whirled away, "that I am the holy priest of Tir, whose wrath *you* have incurred! Let the destruction of the dun fall upon *your* head!"

Indi walked out of hearing, his fists clenched, his teeth set on edge in his anger. The hot sun added to his vexation, and when a hound attempted to run alongside him, it got a swift kick in the ribs in response. He regretted it even as he did it, but he did it anyway, wishing it was Angog—wishing, almost, that it was Tir.

He made his way to the pool in the woods, hoping to relieve his pent-up anger. Thern joined him silently, wisely keeping to the rear. But within the forest the air was even hotter and staler, and Indi found little comfort in the solitude. His chest seemed cramped and the pain of anger and despair wrenched a hole in his heart. The fear of the horse god made him tremble, and he wondered, really wondered, would the dun come to ruin because of him? In his mind's eye he saw the brown of the crops, he smelled the smell of famine. And it was because of himself. He knew that, surely, even when he had tried to thrust the blame off on Procyon. He, the Chieftain's son, was a friend of the heretic holy man.

Of course it was his fault, he told himself with a sudden quiet clarity. Yet, for all that, he could not bring himself to renounce Procyon's friendship. Procyon, who was all friendliness and certainty, like a lantern on a winter evening. There was all foolishness in his talk, even as Angog had said, but for some reason Indi could not explain, he could not bring himself to push Procyon's words away for good.

He stopped on the edge of the river and looked at his dancing reflection. His hair was long and ruddy-coloured, his skin healthy and rippling with a man's tattoos. He had scars of hunting on him and the fierce, unmistakable pride of a chieftain's son in his face. He had no mirrors, but the river served well enough, and Indi knew what sort of man he was: he was handsome, well-trained in war, and ready to take his place as Chieftain of the Downland dun. But—what sort of man was he *really*? Did he make his own way, or was he shaped by the gods he followed? And would he be as Angog was, following Tir, or like Procyon, whose God scorned the bones of animals and the phases of the moon?

It was a question he could not answer.

Thern got to his feet just as there was a snap and a clicking of twigs behind him. Whirling round, Indi saw Cynr come out of the woodshore, and for a moment he was not sure he was happy to see the other.

"Cynr…" he began and fell silent.

Cynr stepped up, his new bow in his hand. Thern stretched out for a pat, but the young man did not take any notice of him. There was something in his face, something behind his eyes that Indi just caught the tail of before Cynr pulled the veil across and he was himself again.

"Indi … I bring good news."

"Do you?" Again Indi was unsure he was glad to be listening.

Cynr flashed a sudden smile, reddened, and went to look into the river himself. Indi stood by him, wondering, as their reflections rippled back up to them, what sort of man Cynr really was. He waited patiently for the answer to his question, watching the light springing from eye to eye in his friend's face like a dancing candlelight. But even with the light, the veil was still there.

"Indi, now you and I are brothers—or very nearly," he said at length.

Indi held up his hand, turning the wrist upward to the light and revealing a long silver scar. "Of course we are brothers, Cynr," he frowned. "We mingled blood years ago."

Cynr shook his head and crouched down, his arms folded across his knees. He seemed to have trouble telling Indi what he meant. "Nay, not like that. I mean Lenag."

Indi stiffened. "Lenag?" he repeated his sister's name dumbly.

Cynr looked up, suddenly afraid. "You do not approve, brother?" he asked anxiously. "Matheorex said you would approve."

Indi shook himself and crouched down by his friend. "Of course I do!" he replied quickly, without really thinking. "Tirna Mother will be pleased."

And yet, there was something that nagged at the back of his mind, something urgent, which tasted almost like fear.

In the eveningtide before the celebration, Indi stood with the rest of the warriors in the courtyard at the foot of the dun. The sky was going dark and the bats were out whirling in the black, their soft cries pricking the night's fabric. For once he was glad to be a space apart from Cynr, standing in the background with the other young men. Beside them the bonfires stood, ready to be lit. They would be kept burning through the night to keep the bride fertile through the night; if the fires went out, the girl would have no children. The maids were moving among the bonfires now, putting the last bundles of wood in place.

The evening had whirled around him like one of the bats, a confusing blur of eating and drinking and laughter, which had left him feeling detached from it all, looking at it as though he were looking at a veil, knowing that underneath the excitement was the knowledge that the rains would not come in time. The taste of fear lingered in his throat still.

There was a sputter and burst of flame on his vision, and he came back out of his reverie to see that the maids had lit the bonfires and that the courtyard was beginning to flood with red light. As the fire took and sprang higher, the body of warriors moved forward, Indi with them, jostling shoulders with Tadc and Llyeln, the slight Roman-bred lad, up the crooked lane to the foot of the gravel and timber stairs below his father's house. There was another pause. Cynr stood forward and everyone looked with him to the head of the stairs.

Presently there was a movement beyond the boar-skin door flap. A bat weeked and wheeled in the torchlit darkness. Then the skin flung back and Tirna stepped out, unfolding herself from the doorway, and stepped aside. Matheorex came out next, his frame filling the entryway, his red hair ablaze in the light. And Indi found himself holding his breath, waiting for the last figure.

Lenag was a beautiful bride. Her gorgeous golden hair with its red highlights was caught up in a layered crown about her head, the little ringlets falling down about her ears. She had washed so that her skin glowed like almonds, her feet were shod with doeskin sandals, and her breasts seemed to quiver with excitement. The fabric his mother had bought had been for the wedding dress, and she stood decked out like a candle, flaming and lovely. And at her throat, pulled up to the creamy hollow of her skin, he saw the familiar image of the beaded sword. The sight of it jolted the world into startling clarity out of the hazy yellow smoke.

He was suddenly aware that Procyon had slipped to his side. There was no time to say anything, but he could see in the other's face the same fear that he was tasting himself, and he knew it was for Lenag, but he was not sure why. What did the heretic holy man see, he wondered, that provoked him to hand over his beaded sword, which was precious to him, no matter what little power he professed it held?

His attention was drawn by Cynr's ascension of the stairs to stand before Matheorex, who took his hand and Lenag's and held them up to the sky. And then he remembered what was coming next and he braced, suddenly appalled. Angog appeared out of the house behind them, knife in hand. Lenag's eyes were cast down; Indi could see her face was white. Tirna held the great copper-worked goblet of wine beneath the two hands, and Angog, chanting as he worked, set the blade to the two wrists and gave them a merciless slice. Lenag did not flinch, and for that Indi was glad.

Tirna caught the blood in the cup and handed it to Matheorex, who, after speaking the invocation, "A blessing upon the son born into my family, a blessing upon him and his sons," handed it to Cynr. Cynr took it and drank with a reckless toss of his head, flashing a smile as he pulled the cup back down and handed it across to Lenag. More demurely, Lenag drank, still without flinching, draining the cup. Then, the ceremony over, Cynr lifted up his bride and ducked into the houseplace, leaving the rest of the dun to finish out the night's feast.

When he remembered to look for Procyon, Indi saw the man melting away through the crowd. He frowned, feeling oddly as though something were being wrenched away with him, but as he put out a foot to go after the man, he saw his mother come through the press toward him.

"Indi," Tirna murmured, looking up into his face questioningly. "Is something wrong?"

"Mother," said Indi a little crossly. And he was not sure what was wrong, only he knew that everything was wrong. "I am thinking about the rains and the crops," he said, which seemed the obvious answer to make. Then, harshly, "I am wishing that Tir would stay down in his Holy Place and leave our lives peaceful. I fear I hear Tir's hoofbeats on the chalk track coming this way."

Nodding sadly, Tirna pulled her mantle around her thin shoulders. "Son," she whispered, "I hear them coming, too."

THE IMMORTALITY OF THE SOUL

INDI DID NOT SEE LENAG until several days afterward. Bandr the colt, pastured out on the Downs with his mother, had colic for a few days and demanded constant attention, so when Indi was finally allowed to return to the dun it was with heavy steps and a head ready to sleep. Thern tagged along behind, drifting aimlessly from side to side, often stopping to sniff a beetle, or startle a crow, or water the turf.

Indi watched the last crow fly off with weary eyes. But even in his weariness he noticed that there were more crows than just one now. They congregated down by the fields, and while the boys were busy chasing them off, their work was mostly in vain. *Tir,* Indi thought. *It is Tir's work*. That knowledge settled in a pit of despair in his empty belly and a cloud descended over his spirit. He wanted to talk to Procyon again, but he had not seen the little brown man since the marriage ceremony.

The sky was clear still, bereft of a sniff of rain from east or west, and the soft wind was kicking up a thick cloud of dust along the road. It was a heavy, suffocating mist that Indi struggled through to gain the dun, and when he did make it through, he was covered from head to toe in fine white chalk. His hair was dulled by the dust, and even his lashes were caked with the road's sweat.

"Indi map Matheorex, you are a sight, though not for sore eyes. You'd make eyes sore."

Indi pulled up and turned to face the speaker. "Procyon!" he cried, flashing a tired smile. "I had wanted to see you."

Procyon made a surprised expression. "Did you really? Well, someone else enjoys my company. That makes for good hearing."

"Oh?" asked Indi, slapping off the sides of his tunic. "Who else enjoys your company?"

"Your sister enjoys my stories. She seems to understand the meaning behind them."

Indi nodded slowly. "So. That is why you gave her the beaded sword."

Procyon smiled, his dark eyes twinkling. "Aha! You saw that? Yes, that is why I gave the beaded sword to her. I find she is not so very proud as many around here. I think God answered my prayers in her."

The young man frowned sidewise at the little brown man. "What prayers did you have concerning her?" he asked, warily sniffing holy portents in Procyon's words. "What have you to do with my sister?"

But Procyon only smiled, smiled like a girl who had been kissed. "She is a child of my God," he explained. "She is a follower of the Christos."

"A follower of the wooden sword, you mean?" Indi asked. "You mean, one of your kind? My sister?"

"Hush, Indi. Yes, one of my kind. But don't worry; we don't eat people alive or wreak vengeance on our wrong-doers. That is not our way. Our God takes care of us."

Indi looked up at the quiet house. Surely no holy hoof had smashed the roof beam in yet, but the gods knew....

"You still don't understand, do you?" the little brown man asked softly.

Indi looked back at Procyon, his dusty brows drawn together, making a dark cleft between them. His eyes were shadowed and confused. "I don't understand anything," he replied after a while.

"Nothing makes sense to me, not Tir, not Taranis, not Christos. All is confusion and—and foolishness."

"Yes," Procyon's face suddenly clouded with sadness. "I pray and pray, and teach and teach, but the word of the wooden sword—the cross—is still foolishness to those who are perishing. Only to us whom God has seen fit to save is it power. You see, Indi," he looked up. "God's foolishness far exceeds the greatest wisdom of any seer. And yet, to man, it still seems foolish. I know I should not wonder that Lenag has become a Christian, for my God said He does not call many wise and noble, not many wealthy or well-off—"

"Lenag is the daughter of a Chieftain!" Indi objected hotly.

Procyon looked even more sorrowful, and even Thern gave a whine, thrusting his wet muzzle into the leathery palm. His tail thumped the ground. "The wooden sword, Indi, the cross," he said. "There is level ground at the foot of the cross."

Indi watched the brown man walk away. Thern whined a little then trotted after him. With the going of the former Indi felt a strange sense of sorrow, and with the going of the latter Indi felt the world had betrayed him. He clenched his dusty hands and spun on his heel, striding up to the houseplace. But though the burning anger that filled his empty soul consumed him, his feet seemed all the heavier now that the world had turned against him. And as he paused under the white scar-mark of Tir above the doorway, he wondered what awaited him within and felt that he did not belong there.

"You really hate me, don't you?" Indi asked the carving.

When nothing happened and the intense silence seemed almost to mock Indi, he drew his knife on a wild impulse and slashed an ashen line through the god. He left quickly, half terrified at what he had done, and strode resolutely into the house. Young Sitag met him, whining like a pup and fawning about his dusty knees. He frowned, not in the mood to love his little sister even in the customary rough, man-like way.

"What do you want?" he asked harshly.

The child looked at him with worshipful eyes. "I'm a black hound puppy," she explained. "My name is Moch-co."

Indi sucked in his breath, his unbelieving eyes darting round to peer in the shadows. "Who named you that?" he inquired, trying to keep his voice steady.

"Cynr did," Sitag cried happily, prancing around Indi.

Indi stared at her a moment, thoughts whirling. Then he bent down and patted his sister's bouncing curls. "Good pup," he said and pushed past her. But he caught something in the air that the cheerful, innocent child did not. Even as he moved forward, the heavy silence of the room engulfed him in a sense of panic. One of the hounds got up from the hearth, whined, and slunk past Indi out the door. Hackles raised, the young man stalked down through the shifting shadows, peering this way and that through the gloom. Nothing stirred, but his body picked up the gentle reverberations of talk. It was not until he reached the end of the room and turned to look into his parent's chamber that he realized what was happening.

There a dismal sight awaited him. His mother, sister, and brother stood round his father's bed, their faces white and worried. By the faint light of a candle Indi could see his father lying on the bed, looking very sick. His stomach turned over and he felt he was going to vomit.

Tirna saw him. "Oh, Indi!" she whispered. "We don't know what to do! It all happened so suddenly."

As Indi walked over to his father he felt like a ghost; his body floated quietly over the ground, and he felt nothing about him, not even when Lenag reached out and touched his arm for a moment.

The pale yellow face of the chieftain lay fixed upon the listless head. The one arm that protruded from the doeskins was also of a saffron hue. Indi bit his lip. *Where had the bronze colour gone?* he wondered. *Where had the power and the majesty vanished as if it were a morning mist?* No one spoke; no one seemed to have anything to say. Indi felt he had to break the silence.

"Have you called Procyon?" he asked.

Cynr laughed harshly. "Why call the brown-skinned holy man when our own can do no good?" he retorted. "Isn't it because of Procyon that our father is ill?"

The knife slash! Indi felt sick again. Had he done this to his father? "When?" he asked quickly, ignoring Cynr's words. "When did this happen?"

"Two days ago," his mother replied. "He would not rise from bed, and his water is dark. Nothing we have given him has done any good. I fear ... Tir's hoofbeats ..." Her voice trailed off.

His father was dying. He knew that suddenly, very coldly and clearly. Tir was taking his father away slowly and painfully, not with the sudden smash of his hoof through the roof beam. And he found himself wondering where his father's spirit would be taken and had the sudden image of a wolf dragging a felled buck into the undergrowth of the forest, its lips bloody all over as it tore at the body ...

"Indi—," Lenag whispered.

Indi turned and left the room, unable to hold the gentle gaze of his sister. Hers was the only expression of peace in the house, and Indi could not stand it. It was Procyon's doing, and deep down inside, Indi was furiously jealous. Why was he the only one tormented by these waves of thought: what sort of man a man was, whither the man went after death, what sent him there?

He passed young Llyeln on his way down the stairs, hearing the other's murmured welcome only clearly enough to jerk a hand in reply. He noticed no one else until he found himself stopping under a lone poplar. He gazed up through the branches at the clear sky, his face hot with indignation. His strong hands grasped the tree until his knuckles turned white. "You hate me, I know you do!" he shouted, not sure who he shouted to. "Why can't you leave us humans alone? Leave us to our lives! Stop clouding my path with questions whose answers you hide from me!"

He looked back down at the fields, his breath spent, his anger spinning out. He sighed. This was life, this was how it would always be; what was the use of yelling at the sky? Angog did that, and look where it got him. Indi slid down and sat against the tree, one arm still around Thern, but more for support than in the desperate need to strangle something. In the peace of the outdoors, after he had had his say to the gods, his mind was clearer, and he began to think logically again.

"Surely there is something that brings the rain and the dry," he said to a little ant toiling by his foot. "Look, even you find food to eat. Who watches over you? Surely not the gods. They are almost too busy and unfeeling to care for us. And when they touch us, it is to kill us." Indi looked to the field again, his throat constricting when he saw how very brown and hopeless it was. He whispered to the ant, whispered so the gods would not hear. "What if the Brown Voice speaks rightly? What if there is only one supreme God, and all the rest are evil fakes?"

Indi ducked his head between his knees and ground his teeth in despair. "Where will I find my answers?" he cried.

THE HOLY PLACE

The reeds by the river were crooked and brittle. The water itself was hot, sluggish, as despondent as the young man who sat on the river's banks. The only puff of wind was his sigh.

"Father is worse every day," Indi remarked to Thern. "And the crops … even the horses are cross." The dog whined softly. It was as if the animal understood. Indi patted his rough wolfish head.

There was a crack behind him which made him sit up and swing about silently. There was a series of more cracks and swishes, and Indi knew at once who it was. No one in the dun would make so much noise walking through the woods. It had to be Procyon.

The little brown man staggered through the brake, mopping his brow. He was out of breath and red-faced, but Indi could not say that he was an unwelcome sight.

"You have been gone a long time," Indi accused.

Procyon sat down next to him, dipping his dusty feet into the warm water. Clearing his throat, he said, "Yes, I am afraid so. I thought that until the dun got accustomed to Matheorex being ill, I should melt into the shadows."

"Whatever for?" Indi demanded. "Are you afraid?"

Procyon looked at him sharply. He was not angry because his dignity had been offended but because Indi had the audacity to think such of him. Deep inside, Indi knew the Brown Voice was not afraid.

"Indi, that is not the case," he said sternly. "There are some in the dun who need me, and I thought that being killed by a mad priest was not a wise thing at present. Even you need me."

Indi was quietly pensive for a few minutes. "Yes," he nodded. "I do need you. I need to know: what sort of man am I?"

Procyon sighed. "You have heard this over and over, my son. You are a sinner, like all the rest."

Indi's face flushed. "Am I as bad as—as Cynr?" he demanded, half startled at himself for saying it but mostly angry. Little things, oddly harsh things, had come out of Cynr of late, directed at Lenag. A scornful glance, an oppressive silence—small things that left Indi bewildered and smarting, and he wondered if it all had to do with Procyon's God and the little beaded sword Lenag wore about her neck. "Would I mistreat my wife, would I forsake my hound? Would I break all moral ties?"

There was a quietness about Procyon as he answered and that peace that Indi coveted so passionately. "My dear Indi, it is not my place to determine which of you is worse. Quite frankly, heaven sees you alike in that you have both denied from your earliest stages of life the sovereignty of God and have not offered up due worship to the one Godhead. Only a single sin breaks you from the holiness of God. And you have sinned, been born to sin, so you are as much a sinner as Cynr is, though perhaps you have not sinned so much. But you could. You have it in you; everyone does."

Indi clenched his fists tightly. What he wanted to say was so hard he felt he could not do it, but he felt his body would rend apart if he did not say it. "I … I want to be a man like you, Procyon," he said tightly. He almost glared at the other man, daring him to laugh. "I want that peace you have."

But Procyon did not laugh. Instead, a wild grin full of tears spread across his face. But he contained what appeared to be the utmost bounty of joy. "Indi, do you understand how to get it? You can't just be a man like me, you have to be a man like God."

"The Christos, you mean?"

Procyon nodded solemnly. "You cannot possibly hope to do it on your own. Because Adam—you remember him—fell from holiness, ever since that time there has been a breach between God and man that is, to man, irreparable. But God crossed the breach himself, became a perfect man, and paid man's debt of holiness to God."

"And because of that, following the Christos assures our holiness?" Indi completed quietly. He was not sure he understood. *Foolishness*, the faint voice of the priest whispered. *A Red-Crest sword freeing men*. But somehow there was an unreasonable glimmer of hope in the saying. "What sort of man are you?" Indi asked on an impulse.

Procyon quirked a smile, pondering over this. He opened his mouth in a quick breath then replied, "Indi, it isn't so much what I am *now* as what I trust to the Lord I shall *be*."

"You'd trust your God with your life, Procyon friend?"

Again the shining smile. "Indi, He *is* my life; that is the point."

Indi looked down at his still reflection in the water. The water was so warm, for a moment his stomach churned at the thought of drinking it. It would only make him thirstier. The sun parched his tongue. *Oh!* he thought. *For water that quenched my thirst!*

"I want to think on this carefully," Indi said at last, rising. "There is a lot to think about."

Procyon got up with him. "Of course, Indi. There is indeed a lot to think about: life as opposed to death, eternal holiness as opposed to eternal sin. You know, your gods are under the wrath of mine. I am only thankful that I was taken from under that wrath in time."

Indi nodded and respectfully left the little brown man. The hot sun—which bore hard into the epochs of autumn—was sinking beyond the horizon, but its heat remained like an everlasting reminder of Tir's own wrath. No one had mentioned the slash mark through Tir's image above the Chieftain's houseplace, but Indi had seen the disapproving glances from his fellow warriors, had seen the glare Cynr gave him, had seen even his mother give him a look of shock. Only Lenag had smiled at him in a peacefully encouraging way.

Lenag. Indi glanced up the hillside as he came out onto the track. "I will go talk to Lenag," he said aloud to himself and Thern, who was always close behind. His legs took him swiftly, but it was not swift enough for him to miss the crumpled ears of corn only half grown in their sheaves when, by this time, they ought to have been nearly full. It turned a cold lump in his empty belly. As he ran, he caught the fleeting figure of a white-clad man standing on another hill. It, too, turned his belly.

Shall I never be free of them, the worry of the harvest, the haunting knowledge that I *did this to my dun?* he thought with despair. *Shall I never be free of Angog's eyes watching, always watching from some distance? If the gods commune with such, there is no hope for me should I meet the gods.*

Lenag was not in the houseplace when Indi arrived. Sitag was there, playing with the puppies. She grabbed one living roll of fat and swung it up for Indi to see.

"See?" she shrieked with laughter.

Indi was distracted. "Not now, Sitag. Where is Older Sister?"

Sitag swung the pup to and fro. "Out in the apple garden. See this pup?"

"Cute," Indi assured her. He went out of the building and round to the tiny garden at the back. The sunlight turned the place saffron and crimson, and there was a soft scent of apple-spice hanging in the air. Of all the places in the dun, it was the most pleasant. Though they were small, the apples were hardy and good to eat. But the dun could not live on apples through the long winter.

Lenag was sitting on a wooden bench under one tree, a basket of the fruit beside her. She was sewing a length of dull brown cloth with small patterns of vibrant crimson. It looked like patches of blood on the cloth in the dying light of the sun. It turned Indi's stomach again.

Lenag looked up when her brother approached. Instantly the care on her face vanished into a smile when she saw him. "Indi!" she purred, rising.

Indi beckoned for her to remain seated. He lounged against the tree, watching her work. "I spoke with Procyon today," he remarked.

Again, that smile! "Did you? What did you talk about?"

Indi shrugged. "We talked about … his God. It is in my mind that his Christos is a better God to follow than our own."

The smile disappeared slowly, but Lenag was not upset. She was serious. There was a moment of quiet between them while she seemed to sort out her thoughts; her hands flickered on the fabric in her lap. "Indi, Indi, He is. You know how harsh Cynr can be; but Christos gives me strength for each day and peace when there is none. I couldn't live without Him."

"Then it would be a good choice?" Indi pushed. Why he was asking this information from a woman was beyond him, but he knew that Lenag, of all people, would know. "It is because of the Christos that Cynr is so cold."

Lenag shook her head. "Which do you think would be a better choice: to die in abject humiliation, being your own worthless god in the face of the true One, or to lay down all self in honour of that true God and to live forever serving Him?"

"I should think being a god would be nice," Indi mused. "At least you don't have to worry about what the gods can do to you."

Lenag sighed, her hands listless in her lap. "Oh, Indi," she sighed again. "You can't be a god until you've given up your claim. You know what Procyon has told us: are we not gods? But without submission to the one God, we are just like all those other false gods, and we try to steal the honour and glory of the Christos. But if you are born of a God, doesn't that make you one?"

"After a fashion," Indi admitted.

Lenag went on. "Well, when we become what Procyon calls Christians, people who follow the Christos, then we are born of the Spirit of God into his family, and we become Gods."

"You hardly look like a goddess!" Indi started laughing gently.

Lenag looked at him seriously. "It isn't what I look like now as what I'll look like by and by," she replied with gravity. "Not like the Gods we know now, but as the children of *God*, holy and undefiled, and ruling the world shining like the sun. Can you not see it, Indi? Can you not see what a God's children must be like?"

Her words silenced Indi. His heart pounded with the intense desire to be a God; he had never known it was possible. To rule like a God!

But then Lenag was saying softly, "You've got to give up the claim." She was working again, staring down at her sewing so that they could not see each other's faces. "Give up all and serve Him. Only then will you be given all you do not deserve."

Indi hardly had an answer to this. He leaned against the apple tree, absently watching Lenag's hands working in the westering light. There was a faint wind that made the dry apple leaves rattle, but he could not feel it. The garden, neglected as it was, was a blur of orange and gold light, tarnished into damson where the shadows of the dry stone wall fell. And Indi might have pushed off and gone away from the scene, leaving Lenag to its beauty, taking his thoughts elsewhere. But of a sudden the brazen evening was broken by Sitag screaming in the houseplace. Indi stood frozen a moment, feeling his heart thudding in his chest. Then he shoved off from the tree and was running; Lenag leapt up beside him, sending the apples spilling like rubies across the lawn. But Indi outdistanced her and gained the doorway of the house first, hearing his little sister's desperate screams of "Father! *Father!*"

Indi burst into the house, ruddy hair flying, chest heaving. He came in just as two of his fellows were snatching the girl out from under a bed. They dragged her out on her face and pinned her down. Twisting her head to the side, she caught sight of her brother.

"Indi!" she screamed. "Make them let me go!"

Indi thrust his way in. He sent the first man sprawling with a blow to the temple, and he locked one arm around the neck of the other. Sitag scrambled up and tried to run for it, but a third fellow came out of nowhere and snagged her. Their faces were indistinct, as though he were seeing them in a dream, red through his rage. He did not recognize them as he fought for the terrified little girl.

A hand grasped his shoulder and hauled him back. Indi swung at the intruder, only to get both his wrists locked in a tight hold. It was Cynr.

"What are you doing?" Indi shouted in the other's face. "Let my sister go!"

"Enough!" Cynr shook him hard. "You have done enough damage already. Stand down—Sitag is for Tir."

"No!" Indi cried, struggling with all his might. The bewilderment he had begun to feel toward Cynr for his growing harshness turned to disbelieving hate. "No! She is only a little girl!"

"That makes her the perfect sacrifice," an almond-smooth voice explained.

Angog stood in the doorway, his features black against the darkening sky. The wind had dropped away, but somehow his white cloak stirred softly like a loathsome, coiling snake about his ankles.

Indi lunged at him, teeth bared in unmasked abhorrence; he barely kept down the bile in his stomach. This nightmare had to end. "I am the Chieftain's son!" he cried. "Let my sister go!"

Angog stepped back to allow the men to take Sitag away. She was screaming and howling, and they were not gentle with her. Her white face flashed a look of terror at Indi. There were tears running down her beautiful young face, a picture of the innocence of youth.

"No!" The sound came out of Indi' throat guttural and savage with desperation.

Cynr put a strong bowstring around Indi's wrists. But Indi was too smart for that—too angry for that. The power of rage flooded through him. He flung his arms round, pinning the other's arms to his sides, and landed a breathtaking blow to his abdomen. Cynr doubled over and backed off, and Indi was able to leap to his feet, holding his knife outward.

But Cynr was quick too. In an instant, he had Indi at arrow-point. Both were breathing heavily, shaken, muscles corded and pulsing with tension, eyes wide, mouths crooked open slightly. There was silence between them for moment. Whoever made the first move would die.

"Cynr!" Lenag said sharply, desperately.

Staring into Cynr's eyes up the shaft that would end his life, staring into the face of death, Indi felt something in him change. The bewilderment had given way to hate, and now it gave way to a horrible despair, a despair that wanted to kill just once more before its own destruction. Indi choked on the sensation.

There was a scrabble of claws on the threshold and the patter of sandaled feet. A dark, round, short shape loomed in the doorway. "Indi! Indi, what on earth is happening?"

Indi willed his mouth to move, his tongue to form the words; they came out thickly for his need to be ill. "They have taken Sitag down to the Holy Place to sacrifice her to Tir."

Procyon made a choking sound himself. "Sacrifice her? What for?"

Cynr answered. Indi hated his air of confidence as he spoke. "For the wellbeing of her father," he replied. "Angog has decreed that unless Tir has one of this household, Matheorex will die."

"Why wasn't it me?" Indi asked. His voice sounded suddenly like that of a person who needs water desperately.

Cynr laughed. "You, O defiled one?" he chanted. "Need I answer that?"

Procyon scuffled his feet in agitation. "Drop that bow this instant, you foolish boy!" he commanded. "Come, Indi, let us go down there."

Indi was not sure what compelled Cynr to obey the little brown man, but he saw a confused look pass over his face and the bow lowered to the ground. Indi jumped to Procyon's side, and together they and Thern went racing down the timber and gravel stairs, out of the dun, and down to the accursed, dark Holy Place.

The darkness had just become complete when they arrived. The moon was rising over the eastern hills, and the scent and oppression of evil, mingled with the lost feeling of despair, were bearing down on Indi like a mountain. There were torches in the clearing and a great crowd of people who had come down in the wake of Sitag and the warriors. Tirna was nowhere to be seen.

He was too late. Just as Indi slithered to a halt, he caught sight of the writhing form between the two largest of the torches and that snake-like, arching form of the priest bending over it. The arm went up, flashing with a knife, and came down. The form lay still, and a horrible wailing chant went up, calling the name of Tir. Thunder rolled far off.

He had never seen anything like it, not in the faces of any of the gods. The child, a little girl, killed. The thought repulsed him as much as the blood dripping from Angog's knife. Why? he demanded. Why? What god would do such a thing? What god could be good that men like Angog—and Cynr—would follow in such a brutal, inhumane way? This was not holiness. In that horrible moment of standing there, staring at the knife in disbelief, Indi realized he had been following a lie. It was not true—it could *not* be true!

Sick to his belly and sick to his soul, the young man turned and ran. Thern darted after him, weaving through the shadows. Indi had no knowledge of where he went. All he could see was the flash of the knife and the thunder of Tir's hooves on the air, coming to receive his offering. He heard a scream behind him, distant and awful. Was it Sitag's spirit, crying in pain? he wondered. What use was a dead body? The image of the white horse carving with the gash through it sprang into his mind with jolting clarity. Tir did not want his sister, he wanted an excuse to come down and wrest Indi from the lands of the living. That was the thunder in his ears, the pounding of hooves coming nearer and nearer.

Indi collapsed at the edge of the river, his arms over his head. He was sobbing for breath, ready to wretch his heart up, and lost as to where to go. Nowhere could he hide from the bright god-eyes of Tir. He would find him. The horror of it filled the air. The terror of the realization that all he had called good could, without a thought, rip his soul from his body and drink his blood and be happy for it, filled him with more revulsion than he had ever known. He was an enemy of the gods, and they knew it. He knew they were evil, and they would silence him. He knew they had lied, and they would kill him.

"Will no one help me?" he cried.

Snap! "Indi, for heaven's sake, slow down!"

Indi whirled around. There, a rock amidst the storm, the one unshaken figure that he knew. "Procyon!" he gasped. He reached into the dark and snagged the old man as if he were a lifeline. He pulled the little brown man down beside him. "Procyon, he's coming for me!"

"Who?" Procyon asked. "Cynr is still at the Holy Place. I left to find you as soon as I could—"

"No!" Indi cried, shaking the man as if it would help him understand more quickly. "No, no—Tir! He is coming to find me, to kill me. He knows I hate him, he knows I defiled his image. I know he is evil, and he knows I have discovered this! He won't stand for it! He will kill me to silence me!"

Procyon laid his leathery hands on Indi's bare shoulders. "Indi, you said you wanted help."

Indi nodded, still sobbing like a horse in a fire. His empty belly convulsed. "You are never afraid," he said, struggling to steady his voice. "You have no fear—you said so. I want that. I want some truth I can cling to and not fear that the gods will demand my own soul for their evil pleasures." He dropped his voice to a whisper. "I want to be rid of them."

As though there were nothing to fear, as though there were all the time in the world between them, the other made himself more comfortable in the rushes; and the very gesture, in its apparent absurdity, made Indi feel a little safer. "Indi, I have told you and I have told you. It is the Christos who is the one God, the one you must follow. Do you not remember this?"

Indi remembered this. He remembered, too, that Procyon could not follow a God who was like Tir—evil and demanding—and that the God whom Procyon claimed could not be cruel or unjust. How could such a God be evil if he filled Lenag's and Procyon's faces with such an unearthly glory? A sudden determination, as desperate as it was firm, rose inside him. "The wooden sword," he said thickly. "The cross—I want the power of the cross."

"You want to follow the Christos?"

He lifted his head. "Yes. I'll give up being a god, I'll give up everything! I will follow the Christos. I will follow Him forever. Please, I need the Christos more than anything." But then, even as he spoke in his desperation, a horrible thought came to him. "But what if He doesn't accept me? I am a man just like everyone else—just like Cynr!"

"Of course you are," Procyon assured him with a tone almost of mirth, if that were possible. "Those are the sort of men He calls. Ask, Indi. Ask. He is good."

He is good. Indi bowed his head to the earth and whispered, as if to it. But in his heart he was crying to the highest of heavens. "Christos, Christos, help me—"

THE NIGHT OF GHOSTS

DESPITE THE HEAT AND CLOSENESS of the night air, Indi lay in a cool rapture on his bed, staring up at the dark beams above. He saw nothing but the thoughts of his own mind, and the trample of god hooves did not disturb his soul. He felt free and weightless, like a bird setting itself to flight at dawn. Every night was like this: an erratic, almost physical soaring into the bounds of eternity. His heart soaked up every word the little brown man told him until he felt fit to burst and still he begged for more. Now at last, after so many months of torture and agony, he had that peace he had longed for.

Turning on his side, Indi's eyes picked up the black form that was, in daylight, the door to outside. For a few moments his mind travelled beyond it to the mortal realm. He thought of the dry, flat fields and the meagrely stocked storehouses. Now the harvest had come in, his father was still deathly ill, and life had, outwardly, not changed its appearance at all. But Indi did not see it that way. Rolling onto his back again, he smiled, tucking his arms under his head. "He is good," he whispered to himself. "He is so utterly good."

A soft rustle drew his attention. Thern, lying under his master's bed, sat up and whined quietly. Indi sat up to see who was creeping about in the night, and by the dim red light of the banked fire he saw his sister walking cautiously along, one hand holding her skirt above the straw, the other balancing herself from tumbling nearly to the ground.

"Lenag?" Indi whispered in confusion. His sister turned her head toward him. After the sacrifice she had withdrawn to the fringes of his life and he could not remember seeing her until now. "Lenag, why are you awake?"

She sat down by the hearth and patted Thern's rough head. Her mass of loose hair hung about her face, waving as she moved, so that it came to him that she was rather lovely. "It was too hot," she replied. "I needed to get up."

Indi sat on the end of his bed, his toes playing idly with the straw. "It is rather hot," he mused. "One would think winter would come soon."

Lenag nodded. She sighed and remarked, "You have changed, brother. I wanted to talk to you alone."

Indi smiled crookedly. "Oh yes, I've changed, sister. I am a follower of the Christos now."

Her head came up, and she drew in a quick breath, hands up in a gesture of supreme surprise and delight. Then, letting out the breath, she whispered, "Oh, darling Indi, that's the most wonderful news I have ever heard! Now listen, for I have news for you."

Indi leaned forward, his smile still playing on his face.

"I have discovered that I am going to have a baby."

The young man leaned back, his smile even broader. It did not occur to him yet that it was Cynr's child. To him, it was Lenag's child and Lenag's alone. Cynr had no claim to it, even if he had helped make it. To Indi, Cynr had given up a claim on anything the day he sold Moch-co. And it seemed fitting, so soon after Sitag's death, that Lenag should be announcing that she carried a child. "Surely," Indi said, "this is wonderful news. You must be the happiest woman in the dun now."

Lenag brushed her hair out of her face. "Yes," she replied slowly. "I suppose I must be." Then, looking up with a pale face, she whispered harshly, "Indi, I'm worried about it. What if the famine continues and I don't have enough milk to feed the baby? What if it—dies?"

Indi reached out and laid a strong hand on his sister's shoulder. "Hush, Lenag," he said sternly. "If it worries you very much, take your question to Procyon. He will know an answer. But I think you ought not worry. The Christos will look after you."

The young woman took her beaded sword into her hand and played with it thoughtfully. The dull firelight danced darkly off the red jewels. They both looked at it for a long time in silence, thinking each their thoughts. Lenag broke the silence gently. "Cynr says that there is going to be a spirit-burning."

Indi looked up. He had forgotten that Samhain was coming. Images of the bonfires on the Downland hills came to him, images of the ponies shying near the fires, of the scattered bones crackling in the heat, of the heat on his face. He had never been fond of the oppressive dark of Samhain nor of the feeling of death that surrounded it. But this year would be different. This year, in many ways, it would be worse; and in others it would be better, for the Christos had broken the power of death, and the fires would hold no sway over him.

When he failed to make an answer, Lenag silently got up and went back to her bed, and Indi was left to roll back into his.

On Samhain day, Indi went down to the stables with Thern and took out Cisha, Bandr still at her heels, and rode out along the lonely hills to get away from the dun. His father grew steadily worse, Angog's gaze steadily hotter, and he found himself needing to get away into the quiet now and then. So he got away, riding along the windy crests of the hills with the land spread out around him, watching the progress of the bonfire builders in the distance as he idly rode along.

Thern began to bark. Turning around in his seat, Indi heard the rumble of unshod hooves coming over the hard turf. Cynr was riding toward him on a grey gelding, his bare legs thumping steadily against his mount's flanks. Indi's face clouded. The thought of Cynr's company left an evil taste in his mouth and the little flame of hatred still burning in his chest for what Cynr had allowed to be done to Sitag. It was wicked, plain and simple, and he hated it. *Blessed is the man who does not walk in the counsel of the wicked, nor stand in the path of sinners,* he thought to himself; then into the mare's ear, "Hush, hush, Cisha." Bandr gave a short squeal of terror and kicked up his little hooves at the larger pony.

"Hullo, Indi," Cynr said as he pulled his mount up.

"Hullo, Cynr," the young man replied.

They sat looking at each other in silence, each not sure what to say. The evening when Cynr had held Indi back from saving his sister from an awful death lay open before them, filling their thoughts. A prick of guilt pulled darkly at Cynr's face, twisting one side of his thin mouth back and down. The eyes glittered beneath the brows.

Finding a welcome diversion from the past offence in Bandr's crazed gallops into the field and then back to the safety of his dam, Cynr said, "He is growing, the little colt is. Will I have him after the breaking this spring?"

Now Indi was compelled to speak. He would much rather have sat and stared at his friend, wondering at the utter mutilation of his spirit. After a long, drawn pause, he replied quietly, "I recall promising my black colt to my favourite brother, but I think—" he paused again. "I think my favourite brother went east with Moch-co."

Cynr's face reddened with rage. "You have never forgiven me for that, have you, Chieftain's son?" he spat. "Was selling my old hound so heinous a crime that you have estranged me?"

Indi shook his head sadly. "No, not so much a crime," he replied. "You estranged yourself, Cynr. There was something inhuman in what you did. That is what sits so distastefully in my belly—among other things."

Cynr wheeled his pony about. Shooting a dark look over his shoulder, he said, "See then if I care for the black braggart!" He struck his pony's flanks with his heels, producing a sharp scream, and thundered back toward the dun.

Indi sighed deeply. "So much for that," he mused. Whistling up Thern, he decided to survey the fires himself.

The red mare flew along the ground like a dull-crimson cardinal, her small hooves making a cloud of thunder that bore them on. She winged over the burnt grasses and shrivelled wild flowers until, at last, she topped the hill and stood on the flat, poised like a doe against the skyline, and Indi could look out at the long bonfire. It cast little light in the fierce gleam of the noonday sun, but Indi could not see how its tenders could bear its double-portion of heat. It would still be hot when the evening came, Indi thought, gazing up at the clear sky. There was no escaping the heat.

Once again the roll of hoofbeats drummed in his ears. This time, however, it was only a group of young men coming to meet him. Indi sat rigid in his seat, watching quietly as they came up.

Tadc-Hound hailed him. "Indi!" he cried. "We were looking for you. We lads were heading down to the river for a dip. Care to join us?"

Feeling in no way compelled to join them and wondering that they even went out of their way to accost him, he replied, "No, thank you, Tadc. Ride you on without me."

The other looked bewildered. "But are you not hot?" he asked. "Surely you will come."

"Surely I will not," Indi insisted, shaking his head. He was gleaming with sweat from head to toe, but he held to his decision.

One of the other lads cocked a sly smile. "Indi map Matheorex has been quarrelling with Angog. Or maybe he has a woman and he just wants us to go away so he can go see her."

Indi's face creased into an intense frown. To make a retort was to defend the lie, but he ached in letting the statement go unchallenged. But someone did it for him. It was little Roman Llyeln, only three years into his manhood, who spoke up sharply, "Let the Chieftain's son be. You know, when he is Chief, he might not be so quick to forget all your words."

A swift, collective look passed over the men's faces. Indi, watching, saw that it was a mixture of both fear and resentment. It was the resentment that made the skin on the backs of his legs prickle uncomfortably.

Tadc turned his pony about. "Very well. Are you coming, Llyeln?"

Llyeln shook his head. "I think I will stay with Indi map Matheorex. You lads go on."

The others whipped up their mounts and went on after Tadc, and Indi was left with Llyeln on the Downs with the empty wind and the heat all around them. Then Llyeln said, "I fear I forgot to ask you if you felt like company."

Indi quirked a smile. He was glad for Llyeln's show of friendliness as one starved for food. "I am not minding you staying," he assured the other.

Llyeln changed the subject as swiftly as the dart of a kingfisher, motioning toward the fires. "Are you going tonight?" he asked.

Indi nodded. "I was planning on watching, yes. I cannot say I will enjoy it, though."

Llyeln gave Indi an odd look over his shoulder then surveyed the fires with a shiver. "I think we two are in the same camp. I am not certain I will enjoy it, either."

For a moment Indi felt a rush of warmth toward the younger man, hoping there was more beneath the remark. "And why do you feel this?" he asked gingerly.

The other merely shrugged. "I do not know. It is in my mind that the gods are gods and we are but men, and the two coming together is not altogether pleasant."

Hopes dashed, Indi fell silent. "Why go, then?" he asked presently.

Llyeln turned the question back on him. "Why go yourself?"

Indi shrugged. He had some confused notion of facing what had made him fearful all his life, of facing it and knowing it could not harm him. But it was a thing he could not explain. "I have my reasons," he said after a long pause.

The dark head slipped to one side, the dark eyes flashing at him. "Is it that you have a woman?"

Indi suddenly laughed; but it was a hollow laugh. "No!" he cried. "Far from it."

There was another awkward silence, this time from Llyeln's quarter. "I ... I was there the other day when the priest took your sister to the Holy Place. I did not understand. It seemed to be a wicked thing to do. Maybe that is why the fire-burning sits ill in my belly today. But then, Tir is the god."

Indi shook his head. "Hard as it is to accept, he had a claim over my sister," he said softly. Looking over his shoulder at the dun, he knew that nearly every soul therein belonged, as a slave, to Tir, and the evil god could do with them what he willed. What a relief it was to belong to a good God!

"Are you just going to sit here and watch the fires burn?" Llyeln asked. "Or are you going to do something?"

Indi shook his head to clear it of his thoughts. "We could go hunting down in the wood until sunset. What do you think?"

Llyeln gave Indi his broad smile. "Noticed by the great Indi map Matheorex! It is a day of fine things for me. I will come, and I will hunt with you."

Indi gave a small smile in exchange for the wide one. He had nothing to say, so he kept quiet. It was a new thing to be looked up to and not scorned for the slash he had made in the white form of Tir or for his friendship with Procyon. They rode down the hill together, Thern warming to the hunt. They hunted until the sky was dark and the sun was gone, and Indi found the youngest of his former companions to be a warm, companionable fellow, if pagan, and was almost happy. And as the light went out of the sky, together they packed up their spears and the few fat rabbits they had snagged and returned to their hill to sit once more watching the fires.

By this time there was more activity around the flames. Forms moved black and red-lined back and forth, tossing more brush into the fires. A drum began to beat slowly, ominously, its noise rolling out across the hills and valleys of the Downs like the sound of many hooves. The stark blazes of firelight flashed brilliant and eerie across the grass, wavering like insane dancers; bowing, dipping, doubling back on themselves in erratic and sensual poses. Indi turned his head away and tried to survey the stars. For a moment the memory of the light was emblazoned on his eyes, then his sight cleared and he was looking up into a vast expanse of infinite darkness and a myriad of lustrous stars. *The mantle of God*, he thought to himself. *How perfect and untouchable!*

Suddenly a horn yelped wildly, adding its tremendous voice to the drums. A shout went up; Cisha spooked and wheeled on her hind feet.

"They are calling everyone to the fires!" Llyeln said, his eyes wide, taking in the enchanting glow of the fires. He kicked his pony to a gallop and rushed across the flat to join the others. Cisha jumped in behind, but Indi held her back tightly, slowing her to a hesitant trot. His brows pulled down to shadow his eyes, almost as if to create a hood or covering. His half naked body felt exposed to the glare of the fire. What if those fires were eyes? What if they were watching him—who else would they watch?

Shaking aside these silly, womanish thoughts, Indi pulled Cisha to a firm stand and sat turned sideways so he could watch without being in the way. Now a large crowd had formed, making a crescent shape in front of the fires, waiting to pass through between the fires. Beyond the fires was the empty black of the Downs, and it felt as if it were an abyss into which one could fall forever and ever.

The horn stopped yelping and the drums thundered to a halt. There was complete silence, save for the crackle of the ravenous fires. Between the people and the fires—both bonfires being so close, they were all but one—stood the white-shrouded priest, whose pure garments were but a mask over the rotten filth of blood within. Angog was holding aloft an oaken staff in his hand.

"Come between the fires!" the priest said, sweeping the staff before himself. "The old year is burning away. Come between the fires and be purged. Indi! Indi map Matheorex! Come and pass between the fires!"

There was silence afterward. At first, Indi thought he was imagining it, the surrealism blurring the priest's image into moony gold between the flames. But then he knew he was not imagining. It was Tir calling him, challenging him to come out and face him. So Indi got down off his mare and walked stiffly across the lawn to meet Angog. All eyes were watching him intently, but all he saw was a dark hedge of red-lit faces, their bright eyes gazing at him like little animals staring out from the forest.

It seemed an eternity before he got there, but at last Indi was staring into the snapping eyes of the priest. He pulled back his shoulders, facing the figure of blurred moony gold. "Tir calls?" he asked.

Angog smiled. "Tir has chosen."

And it came to him, very clearly out of the blur of fire and pale gold, very brightly like the stars, that this was it. Now was the moment when he told them, all of them, that Indi map Matheorex was a follower of the slain God, the Christos, the enemy of their ways. He noticed, too, that Angog's eyes were oddly dilated and animated, as though it were not only Angog who looked out at him. He resisted the urge to touch his tongue to his lips. "I will confront the god if I must," he said in a surprisingly steady voice, "but I will not pass between the fires."

Angog's eyes came open even more widely. "You will go between the fires. The dun will be purged of your plague!"

They had been standing almost between the fires all the while; the heat of the flames had been smarting on his skin. It blurred and confused Indi's vision so that he did not see anyone coming until he was hit from behind and was sent spinning sideways toward the dark between the leaping flames. With a cry he struck back, grabbing with his left hand. His assailant tried to pull away, to fling Indi through the doorway between the flames and stay behind, but Indi had such a powerful hold that both he and the stranger went tumbling through together. The Chieftain's son landed hard on his side and spun over, ready to defend himself. To his shock and anger, he found Cynr bending over him, a look not unlike Angog's on his face.

"You did this!" Indi cried.

"Yes, Indi, I did this," Cynr replied hotly, breathing heavily. "And I would not have come through if you had not been a fool."

Indi sat up and grabbed his knife to defend himself if Cynr tried anything further. "I refused to go between the fires. I do not believe in the power of the fires; this will have no effect."

Cynr laughed. "Well, I do have faith in them. Perhaps my coming will chase away the evil spirits—and you!"

Hands went round Indi and pulled him upright. It was Llyeln. "Here now, Indi, don't get in a fight. There's going to be drinking and the gods know what, and you might get yourself killed."

"Stay away!" Angog shrilled. He thrust up his arms toward the dark heavens. "Stay away from him, he is cursed! Let the fires purge him!"

Llyeln's face clouded a little. Indi stared back at him and Cynr. Clearly the latter believed Angog, but the young man of Roman blood was not so sure. His eyes seemed to say hesitantly, "Well, you don't *look* cursed...."

Cynr got to his feet and jerked away from Indi, making the crescent sign with his fingers to ward off evil. His eyes showed intense hate and the malice of the gods. Feeling as if in a different world, Indi backed away.

"Fly, Indi," Llyeln whispered suddenly, his face pained for Indi's sake. "Fly! Let the heat sink."

Indi whirled and let himself be swallowed up in the darkness. A pony screamed after him; Angog's voice rent the sky like a knife. The whole world was turning upside down, and his heart was somewhere in his throat while he walked swiftly through the burnt turf in the black, hardly knowing where he was going; he could feel it pounding to get out. Any moment now it would.

Funeral Pyre

When Indi awoke after that dreadful night of living nightmare, it was to find Procyon and Lenag sitting next to him. When she saw he was awake, Lenag held out a bowl to his lips. "Drink, brother," she whispered sweetly.

Indi felt the bowl jar against his chin. The scent of fresh milk filled his nostrils. Hunger roared in his belly. Opening his mouth, he let the translucent liquid pour into his mouth and a little out the sides. Swallowing, he managed a sigh. He felt rather weak; he did not know how far he had run last night with his head feeling as light as air, his heart bursting from his body. He had been running in a dream, and all he knew was that he had to get away from Angog and that horrible look on Cynr's face. *Was Tir worse than these?* he wondered.

Procyon laid his hand on the young man's forehead. "How are you feeling, my son?" he asked.

"I feel better," Indi replied truthfully. "Though I think I am not yet recovered."

"It was a horrid thing." Lenag shook her head. "I hardly believe that it happened."

Procyon took the bowl away from the girl and set it on the ground. "I believe it," he said curtly. "What made you go there, boy? It was very foolish of you."

Indi gave the brown man a quick snarl. "I had to meet Tir," he defended himself hotly, trying to put his reasoning into words. "I couldn't run from him forever."

"Well, you ran fast enough last night."

Indi turned his head into his blankets and shut his eyes. He did not answer aloud, but in his mind he said with a rueful passion, *That was from Cynr. That was from Angog. That was from men.*

A soft, uncertain shuffle sounded near the door. A moment before, Indi had been vaguely aware of footsteps coming up to the doorway and now, opening his eyes, he saw the figure of a young man. The hair was black and stood up on his head as if a mischievous breeze had come and played with it. He stepped in further.

"Excuse me, sir, may I come in?"

Procyon rose and took away the empty earthen bowl. "Certainly, my son."

Llyeln entered, looking about him warily as if he expected someone to jump out of the shadows and take him down. But seeing no one, he gained courage and came closer, offering an apologetic smile.

Indi sat up and swung his bare legs over the side of the bed. "Llyeln," he said briskly and blinked back his sudden dizziness.

Llyeln brightened at the sight of him. "You *are* here!" he cried. "I was afraid the gods had made off with you. How are you?"

"I'm getting along. And you?"

Llyeln made a seat for himself on the floor. "Well," he groaned as he sat down, "I admit I was fairly shaken up about last night's proceedings. I almost wish now that I hadn't gone at all." He looked up narrow-eyed at Indi. "Are you really cursed?" he asked. His tone was one of interest, almost excitement. Indi hated to disappoint the younger man.

"No, Llyeln," he replied heavily. "But Tir does hate me. Perhaps more than he hates Taranis."

Llyeln's eyes grew wider. "It's amazing you're still alive, then!" He lowered his voice. "I heard you slashed Tir's image over the door. Is it true?"

Indi nodded solemnly. "Indeed, I did." He swung his arm out. "You can go look at it, if you wish."

Procyon came back suddenly, shuffling in his brown sandals through the old reeds on the floor. "No time for that!" he gasped, red-faced. "Indi, your father asks for you!"

Indi jumped up, his head now very heavy with reality. His father had called for him plenty of times before, but Indi knew Procyon too well to not understand this time. This time would be the last time. Lenag herself started up, white-faced with shock, but Procyon motioned for her to remain where she was. Only the three men, the young lord of the dun, the little brown man, and the trailing lad with Romanish blood, went to the dark-shadowed bedroom where the mighty old Chieftain lay.

Tirna crouched beside the bed, her head in her arms. One of the household servants huddled in a corner, making the sign of the crescent over and over. Taking it in absentmindedly, Indi knew it would do no good. It was his father's time to die, and, knowing that no shadow of the cross had fallen on the old man, it pained Indi to see him go. And there were no slow, noble words from the old man as Indi stepped to his side. The Chieftain opened his mouth as if to speak, but all that came out was a rush of a cough—a weak cough—and the spirit of the man had departed.

A disbelief took everyone in the room. The servant burst into a wail, thrusting out the crescent at Indi, jerking her hand unsteadily until Tirna, after the shock began to wear away, ordered her out. The servant scrambled up and ran away. Indi never saw her again. He was faintly aware of Cynr coming to the doorway; he could feel the imperious presence of the other man looming over him in disapproval as if the death of the old Chieftain was his fault.

Llyeln stepped aside, breaking the stillness, and held up his hands in salute. "Hail, Chieftain!" he whispered shakily, gazing with bright, wide eyes at Indi.

"He is not Chieftain yet," Cynr growled defiantly behind them.

Indi turned and looked his brother in the eye. Lenag had come up then and stood on tiptoe peering over her husband's shoulder. She looked frightened to death herself.

But Procyon brought the bough of peace between them all before another word could be spoken. He moved to the dead man's side and laid his hand on the face. Tirna cried out, but Procyon only shook his head. "No spirit shall harm me, my lady," he assured her. "Now, we must prepare him for burial. Even if he is a pagan, it is not right that he should be left without an honourable grave."

Indi came to his senses, dragging his eyes away from Cynr's murderous glare. Straightening, drawing back his shoulders, he commanded, "Let my father be buried on the high Chalk where the winds and rain sweep and the world meets the heavens, in the tomb of his fathers. And you are right, Procyon; even if there is no hope, yet honour is his due. I will go now and choose the spot of his burial."

At first Indi was afraid Cynr would not step aside to let him pass, but with one last raking glance, the kind that shot through to the skin, the other moved away, following the young Chieftain with eyes of burning hatred. Llyeln followed like a quiet dog, padding along in Indi's shadow, glancing back with wariness now and again to see Cynr still watching them until they were out of sight.

"Oh!" Llyeln shivered, drawing his red cloak close. "He has eyes like an evil hawk, he does. What bug has made him so irritable?"

Indi walked down quietly to collect Cisha from her stall. He could just see Bandr's slender black head thrusting at the blank sky over the door. Recognizing the scent of his master, the colt brayed sharply.

"I live under the God of the wooden sword," Indi said after a long pause. When he answered, Llyeln gave a little jump of surprise, Indi had been quiet so long. "And Cynr still lives under the horse god. He does not understand my God is the only God."

Llyeln's dark, worshipful eyes travelled after the young warrior. Full of his own thoughts, Indi did not stop to think about what might be on the other's mind. But when he swung astride Cisha, Llyeln kicked up his heels and hurried to fetch his own horse.

The two rode out upon the windy hills. In the west, toward the sunset, the barrows of the chieftains rose against the sky as a great mound of earth, covered over in green turf, its stone-framed doorway gaping at them. Indi left Cisha outside and slipped in, striking a light as he did so. Llyeln, coming in behind him, took the light and held it aloft.

The earthen room was totally silent. The silence seemed to well up at them, thick like a woollen cloth, and the shadows resented being driven back by the lamp. On the stone benches along the walls lay the bones of Indi's ancestors, their shrouds of bright clothing faded and turning to dust. The light pricked out the points of spears and the curve of massive brooches of Hibernian gold.

Leaving Llyeln at the doorway, Indi moved forward down the rows of death-benches toward the back. There were several still empty, and he stopped at the widest of them. It was covered in dust, its foot littered with the wreck of dried turf-flowers. But there was one little spark of yellow wedged between the flags of the barrow floor and, bending down, Indi picked out a little blossom of hawkbit, very dry, but still very lovely. He held it carefully in his hand least it crumble away between his fingers.

Behind him, Llyeln said, "Come, Indi, it is a good place. You cannot keep him above ground forever."

Indi looked round at Llyeln, and he thought the little spark of bloom in his hand was much like the lamp the other carried. "I was looking for my own," he replied.

Llyeln said nothing.

Indi turned away. The bloom fluttered out of his hands and fell to the bench, shattering when it landed.

Matheorex's body was prepared for burial. The ceremonial pyre was erected, and the body of the dead man was passed over it three times then laid to rest in the tomb. When the body was laid to rest on its bed of stone under the dark of the hill, the pyre was lit. Indi held the torch while Tirna Mother wailed the eerie cry of woe into the darkening twilit sky. The smoke stung Indi's eyes as he held it close to the wood but not yet against it. His heart was thumping quietly like a distant drum. The wind changed of a sudden, whispering different times into the young man's ear, and, heeding the words, he lifted his head to the east. Clouds were gathering: black clouds, rain clouds. With a flashing urge he thrust the torch deep into the heart of the pyre and listened as the fire hissed angrily, sank, then caught the tinder and rose like a beacon into the air.

Indi knew the rains would come too late.

CHIEFTAIN SLAVE

IT SEEMED NO SOONER HAD the flames of his father's pyre sunk to an angry, dull glow, shifting in and out of view on the hilltop as the rains drove before the fitful winds, than Cynr was standing in front of Indi, staring levelly into his confused eyes.

They were standing in the Chieftain's old room with its air of death still lingering in the corners like shadows. Now those grey eyes flamed to fierce, defensive blue again as Indi looked Cynr up and down. "Why are you here?" he asked, his hand on Thern's head, who was snarling deep in his throat.

Cynr lounged against the doorway, his eyes wandering round the room a moment. "It is a nice room."

Indi did not answer. He lifted a brow and waited for more.

More came. The eyes darted back to his own, and for an instant the young Chieftain could see something terrible in their depths, something like a knife, and it terrified him. "You are not Chieftain yet," said Cynr again, teeth glinting in the half-light. "Angog has not made you so."

Indi frowned. "I am Chieftain by right of birth," he protested. He lowered his eyes to the wide bed and the chest of his in the corner, to the rug Lenag had braided for Thern, to the bones the hound had been gnawing. "Now, go away and leave me," Indi said at length quietly. "I wish to be alone."

Cynr pushed off from the doorframe and defiantly entered the room, kicking Thern's bone into a deserted corner. In a flash, the hound leapt at the man, teeth bared in a wild sing-song howl.

"Thern! Down!" Indi shouted, grasping after the thick leather collar that just escaped his hand.

Cynr jumped against the wall and bashed the dog away with the back of his hand. His own teeth were bared angrily, his eyes dilated, eyes that were oddly like Angog's. Indi felt the sudden urge to laugh. Cynr gave a quick bark at him the way an annoyed dog will do and said desperately, "You are not Chieftain yet, Indi. We have not forgotten the day the Brown Man came and you fell under his spell. Tir has not forgotten."

"Tir is jealous," Indi heard himself saying, still with that insane desire to laugh, "because he lost me to a greater God."

"May you and your Brown Man and your God perish together!" Cynr roared. He whirled and left the room, but the peace Indi had wanted left with him, and the look of a knife in the shadows haunted him as he sat quietly on the end of the bed, nursing Thern's bruised brow.

A swish disturbed his thoughts. Glancing up, he saw the bulge of Lenag's belly round the doorframe. He had to smile. "You cannot hide, sister. I can still see you."

Lenag stepped into view. Her face was drawn tight with worry; she glanced down the length of the house toward the front door, then she looked back at him. "When you are Chieftain," she asked, "will you forget their words?"

Indi frowned. Llyeln had said mentioned just that once, half candidly, and he had not thought much of it at the time. But he shook his head.

Lenag cast her eyes down to the floor. "What will you do? Cynr hates you to his very black soul—hates me!—"

Indi broke in. "How can he hate my beautiful sister?"

She gestured away with one hand. "Because I am of my brother's people, not his. I am of the Brown Man's people, not his. Because I am not his. . . ."

Indi sighed heavily of a sudden and put his head in his hands, running his fingers violently through his ruddy hair. There was a proud despair in his sister's voice, a sorrowful voice of martyrdom. He noticed that she was wearing a gown sewn with little yellow patterns, patterns like tiny flowers. "Lenag, I can't do this," he said, looking away. "Everything is set against me. How can I be Chieftain when the dun believes I am a curse, when I run from Angog and Cynr, who have set themselves against me?"

Lenag gave him a dark look. She was silent for a long time, thinking carefully on what to say. At last she sniffed softly and replied, "Indi, lord-Chieftain, you *can* face them, and you *can* endure it. Am I not the wife of Cynr? Do I not lie by his side each night and endure his hateful presence? Think of how it is with me! You are a man who can stand for himself. Me? I long for death!" She pulled up her head proudly. "That is the only way to be free of Cynr, to stand before the Christos and be safe forever. You have nothing to be afraid of."

He stared back at her, feeling as though the barrow on the western Downs had opened up in his chest. Bitter, so bitter was that look in his sister's eyes and the weight of her words. And suddenly his own life took on a sweet taste. "Oh, Lenag, I did not mean—" he began, but Lenag suddenly jerked her head around as voices burst through the building. Indi rose and stood beside her, looking out to see none other than Cynr and Angog stalking down between the hearth and bedplaces toward him. There was murder in their eyes.

"Oh, no!" Lenag whispered, sinking into the shadows.

Indi stood up to face them, his brows drawn over his eyes. His legs splayed over the path, cutting off Lenag from Cynr as if—he did not know why, and he did not know what it would accomplish—protecting her from him.

Suddenly Llyeln came running in behind the priest and warrior. He skittered to a halt, face disbelieving. "No!" he cried, starting forward again. "No, you cannot—"

Cynr whirled and brought the heel of his hand up into Llyeln's chin, bringing him crashing painfully to the ground. "Stop!" Indi cried harshly, anger broiling inside him. He had not thought it would come this quickly. "Whatever you have to do, it is with me. You had no right to lay a hand on Llyeln."

"Chieftain—" Llyeln said shakily, getting up and coming to his side.

"He is not the Chieftain," said Angog. He lowered his eyes and swept the two young men up in his gaze. "Tir has shown me his will. Indi has forfeited his right as Chieftain by affiliating himself with the Brown Man, the messenger of Taranis. Cynr is Chieftain."

"No!" Llyeln repeated himself, and, looking at him in that crystal moment, Indi thought he looked far more the man than the boy. "It—you cannot do that!"

Cynr glared at him levelly. "Do you wish to go against the will of Tir?"

To this Llyeln had no answer. Everything pounded in his body against the edict—Indi could see that by the way his face turned red and he ceased to breathe—but he was also loathe to speak against a god. In the end, he let out a drowning gasp and stared at his feet, unable to say anything. The crystal was broken.

Indi turned slowly to his enemies. "So. Do not search for me for a day, and I will be gone."

"It's not as easy as that," Cynr snorted derisively. He came over to Indi and looked intently into his face. Indi looked back quietly. The solemn, almost peaceful look that defied the rapid beats of Indi's heart angered Cynr all the more. He wanted to frighten Indi and frighten him badly. "You've done enough damage to the dun, and you are going to start making amends. You're going to serve me from now on, Indi-*slave*. You'd better not disappoint me."

Thankfully, through all of this, Thern, a wiser dog after his beating by Cynr, merely lay in the shadows with his eyes burning hotly, growling deep in his throat. Indi wondered how to get the dog out safely, wondered what would happen to him. Then it occurred to him in an offhand, distant sort of way, how strange it was that, at a time like this, he was worried mostly about his dog.

"You are quiet," Cynr remarked.

Indi shifted from his thoughts. "What have I to say?" he replied, still quieter. "A slave does not speak unless spoken to."

Cynr's lips curled in a little smile, a smile Indi could not remember ever seeing before. His gaze flickered from eye to eye. Indi could feel Cynr's breath stifling hot against his upper lip. "Tir is god," Cynr said in a low tone. "Speak it."

The young man was faintly aware of Thern's growl getting a little sharper, as if the hound knew the evil of Cynr's words. And then, as the firelight whirled for a heartbeat in Cynr's eyes, Indi knew. Here was the god Tir, and there, in Angog. Parts and portions, yes, he reasoned, but these were the spokesmen of the god he despised, and it turned his heart cold. The sweat gathered on his upper lip, making it still more uncomfortable. His throat constricted painfully until it was all he could do to speak. Cynr was watching like a hawk, Llyeln, half forgotten, was wiggling anxiously where he stood, and Angog was looming behind like a white ghost in his shadows. Their presence was oppressive, and his head felt oddly light and cold. So it surprised him when he heard his own voice, in dead-level earnest, say, "Christos is God."

Lenag let out a strange noise like a strangled man.

Cynr turned away, his face crimson with the scent of defeat. Then he turned back and, in a single swift motion, brought the back of his hand across Indi's cheek. The blow knocked him off-balance for a moment, and he almost lost himself to rage. Then he was able to steady himself and gave back Cynr a look of quiet reproach. Still furious, Cynr raised his hand to strike again, but something stopped him. Indi could see the breath whistling out of Cynr's nostrils: an enraged breath, and he knew the other was searching for a way to hurt him.

"You will be my slave," Cynr said finally, "and all the dun will know it! Llyeln," he snapped the younger man to attention, "go tell them."

Llyeln wavered and sank where he stood. With a dreadful look of apology in his expression he slunk like a whipped dog out the door.

"You will not get away," the new Chieftain said.

Indi lifted his chin calmly. "I will not try to," he replied.

Then he was flying, flying like the wind down the timber and gravel steps, the drum of his heart in his ears. Thern raced along beside him, and Lenag stood on the top of the steps, watching him go. Indi could feel her twisted anguish. *The river*, he thought dimly. *The river!*

Surely God must have been kind to him, for not a soul stopped him in his mad race to gain the riverbank. He crashed like a wounded deer through the undergrowth and nearly plunged over the edge of the river. Then, turning his steps west, he ran for Procyon's favourite patch of reeds with their comic brushes of willow and cat-tail. It was such a peaceful place, it made Indi sick to think of the urgent danger that he brought.

He found the little brown man there, as he hoped he would. Slamming and flattening down the reeds on every side, Indi dropped to his knees and panted out thickly, "Procyon! Run! Cynr—he is Cheiftain—he will have you killed! Run!"

Procyon wasted no time. He was up from the damp ground, dropping his collection of water plants about his sandaled feet. He snapped his fingers once and whistled to Thern. The dog leapt to his side. "I'll take the hound," Procyon said briskly. He kissed Indi's cheeks then said softly, "We'll meet again—here. God be with you."

"And you, Procyon," Indi said, choking through the tangle of his throat. The little brown man slipped off with brindled Thern at his heels, lost in the dappled silence of the water-side forest. And Indi was left alone, desperately alone, to face a life of servitude.

Suddenly Thern was crashing back through the shrubbery, barking loudly. Indi's heart raced. "No!" he whispered, grabbing the hound's collar. He turned the hound about and spanked his rump. "Go with Procyon. Go!"

But Thern was insistent, and it was not until a slip of incredibly thin paper fell out of his collar that Indi understood. He took the paper and held it tightly. Maybe he could read it—Procyon had taught him a little Latin. Thern wagged his tail and gazed adoringly up at his master.

"Go," Indi said, still choking, heart suddenly breaking now more than it had before, now that the reality of their departure came crashing in around him. He pointed into the wood, jerking his arm stiffly. "Go! *Go!*"

Thern whined then turned and trotted away as if he were a wolf. Once again Indi was alone, standing dumbly in the crushed reeds, drowning without a cry in the closeness of his solitude. It was like waking from a surgery, coming up through the haze of shock to a world of fierce pain where every breath was like knives. It was a long time before he could move enough to stare down at the thing in his hands, clutched tightly in his white fists. Like a familiar face or a familiar voice, it steadied him; with a tiny hopeless sound he was able to uncrumple it and look at its inside. Without a doubt the black marks on the paper were from Procyon: fine and defiant, though clearly written in haste. Indi's Latin was far from good, but the sight of it dulled the pain in his chest. It gave him hope.

Shadow Things

INDI GRIMACED AND BRACED HIMSELF under the load. Leg-spread and taut, he strained to lift the two heavy cauldrons of stew. He could feel his back straining almost to the breaking. But he shouldered forward and was careful not to spill a drop. Every tear of stew in those cauldrons was worth three times its weight in gold, he thought. After all, you could not eat gold, and with such a lean harvest ... it was going to be a tough winter.

A gust of cold wind whipped up the dirt aisle of the dun, crashing around Indi. Stopping and lowering his head further, he panted against the strain and bitter chill. Already winter was on its way. Indi knew one thing very clearly: as Chieftain-slave, he would be the last to get a meal in the dun; perhaps even the hounds would go before him. But for all the injustice of it, he found a measure of peace in that little slip of precious paper—a miracle, as far as he was concerned—that Procyon had given him. Late, late into the night he had poured over the incredible words on that paper, struggling to conjure up the memories of Latin words and meanings. Some words he did not know at all but, in its simplicity, he understood. The man had written: "*Whoever wishes to be first among you will be your slave; as the Son of Man, the Christos, did not come to be served, but to serve, and to give his life a ransom for many.*"

Indi had not known the word *ransom*, but he thought vaguely that he perceived its meaning. But the power of the words struck him to the core, and while he knew that there was a greater meaning behind it than just his own earthly situation, it spoke to his heart. So while the wind rushed cold against his bare arms and legs and made him shiver a little and the yoke of his burden rubbed raw across his shoulders, he could find comfort in the knowledge that he was like his God, if only a little. So he pushed on up to the houseplace and stood in the doorway, twisting to get in. The hounds gathered round the hearth growled and moved back as he entered and bent to set down the cauldrons. He let out a sigh as he straightened.

"You are tired, brother?" Lenag asked in a whisper from her side of the fire. She looked round to be sure no one was looking then stooped to fill a bowl quickly. "Here," she urged under her breath; "eat while no one is here!"

Indi took the bowl and drank the thin broth in two gulps and, with a grateful smile, handed the bowl back. "Better wash it; you don't want anyone to know," he admonished.

She nodded quietly and went back to her work as if nothing had ever passed between them. Cynr had more than once over the past few days expressed his deep doubt of Lenag's chastity because she seemed so close to her brother. It had made Indi furious to hear it, to know that Cynr thought that lowly of him, but he bit his tongue and said nothing. Cynr, at least, had not approached him on the matter, and Indi guessed that even Cynr knew it was a lie made to make life miserable for Lenag and that Cynr did not really believe it himself. Indi only prayed that the day would not come when the new Chieftain woke up to find that he did.

Indi turned back at the door. "Where is Tirna Mother?" he asked.

Lenag looked back at him. He was struck with how terribly white, pinched, and hunted her expression was. "She—she is in the back garden, I think."

Indi forced a smile for her sake. "God be with you," he whispered.

Lenag managed something of a smile in return. "And—God be with you, too, Indi brother."

After carefully looking this way and that—like a thief, Indi mused darkly—to see that there was no sign of Cynr on the westward or eastward roads, he slipped round the back of the house and entered the garden. The apple-spice hanging in the air was long since gone, and the poor apple trees were wilting in the rank clouds of winter. There was no saffron glow this particular day, only a chill grey shroud of barely veiled despair. And wrapped against the cold, sitting on the bench, was Tirna Mother: a slim, beautiful figure of chilled grace with her bright eyes dimmed by the passing sorrows that fled before her, dry and brittle as one of the silver apple leaves that scuttled at her feet.

Indi came up to her side and touched her shoulder. She did not turn round or start; she had known he was coming. For a long time she was silent, her head bent to watch one shrivelled crescent of an apple-leaf on the ground. Then she sighed deeply and clenched her hands. "Why, my son, do you do this to us?"

Indi stiffened, his throat contracting as tightly as did her hands. For a moment he found no words to speak, so Tirna spoke in the silence. She looked round at him, her eyes narrow. "I thought you loved your family, Indi. Why have you betrayed us? *Why?*"

Indi knelt and took his mother's hands in his own. They were cold and dry. He gazed into her eyes for a moment. "Tirna Mother—," he began.

"Do not you call me that," Tirna said bitterly, turning her head away. She shook all over.

Indi sighed. So bitter! So bitter, her eyes dark as the frostless sloe-berries. "Mara, Bitter One," he whispered. "Mara, I do love you, so very much. Please believe me."

The shadows of confusion, loss, and despair flashed across his mother's face. "What have you done to us?" she asked, jerking her hands out of Indi's. "You have brought us to destruction—you and your Brown Man." She shivered. "If only I had never dreamt about him!"

Rising and taking the thin face between his large man's hands—strange to think how he had come into manhood so quickly over the past summer and autumn—Indi forced his mother to look at him. Suddenly an urgent fire burned in his eyes as he gazed at her, and a colour sprang to his cheeks like that of anger, but it was not. "Mara, remember your son, Indi? Did he ever do wrong in your eyes?"

"Not my son, Indi," Tirna said resentfully. "I do not know you."

Indi kept to the point, his hold tightening slightly on her face. "Then listen: this new man that came from the ashes of your son Indi will not do wrong but will do *right*, and that is a greater thing."

Letting out a little cry of anger, she pushed his hands off. "You mock me!" she cried. "I want my son!" She glared at him. "I want your God of the wooden sword to give me back my son!"

Indi sat down next to her, and despite her attempts to shove him away, he held her close. "He cannot give me back, Mara," he said. "And I do not want him to. Oh, Mara, Mara! I wish so much that you might know Him!"

"I do not want to know Him!" Tirna shrieked. She broke from his arms and hugged the tree for support. "I do not want to know a God that would steal a son from his mother's very heart and leave her empty."

Indi said, "Your god stole Sitag and killed her and gave nothing in return. My God stole me and gave me eternal life, life beyond the darkness of the barrow and hope to live with Him. He *saved* your son from all that is evil. Can you hate a God like that?"

Tirna looked at her thin hands with their aging wrinkles and tiny, perfect nails. "I would rather my son was dead and buried than walking like a taunting ghost in front of me," she said. "It is cruel of your God."

Indi bowed his head and said no more. A moment later Lenag was calling for him from the steps, and he had to go see what she needed, leaving the shroud of his mother clinging to the dying apple-trees with eyes of bitterness. As he went, heart heavy in his chest, the thick ring round his neck which marked him for a slave banged against his collarbone, producing a hollow sound. He had still not gotten used to the new weight and the way it rubbed his skin. Soon he would have a permanent gall round his neck which would, even if he was released and the thrall-ring was struck off, mark him as a former slave forever. He tried his best to ignore the bitter ramifications of the thrall-ring, but it was hard to swallow.

He stepped up beside his sister on the level before the house-place. "What? What is it, Lenag?" he asked anxiously, seeing the tight excitement in her face.

She thrust a large wicker basket upon him which was meant for carrying brushwood. As she did so, she looked into the basket intently and said under her breath, "Thern is waiting down by the cattle pond—I can just make him out. I think he comes with a message for you."

Indi's heart began to race. He nodded carefully and said slowly, "All right, I will get it for you," and, swinging off, he made his way nonchalantly down toward the forest beyond the cattle pond south of the dun. The Chalk seemed suddenly beautiful and bright to him, and he could make out the brindled pricked ears of his beloved hound sticking just above of the reed-grass round the pond's periphery. Then, as he drew closer, an oscillating tail could be seen behind the ears; Indi hoped Thern would remember himself and not burst out of hiding and begin to bark. Thankfully, he remembered. As Indi came up to the hound, it sunk down at a glance and slithered along the ground beside him, and together they entered the wood. Once well out of sight, Indi dropped to his knees and flung his arms around Thern's neck, digging his fingers into the familiar roughness of his hound's fur. "Oh, you rascal," he whispered harshly into the pricked ear. "How have you been? Have you taken care of Procyon?"

Thern wagged his tail in return, happily licking Indi's face. Indi rose and thumped the hound's flank. "Come," he said, glancing up through the boughs at the sky. "Night is coming on; we had better hurry to meet Procyon."

Being led by Thern, Indi found Procyon at his usual spot on the river amid the reeds. Twilight was lengthening around them, grey and chill, and the birds were fast flying to their nests to huddle down against the cold. Together, the young man and old man crouched side by side, the older one's cloak round them both with Thern lying over their feet.

"It is good to see you again, young Indi," Procyon said with familiar serenity. "How has it been with you?"

Indi nodded slowly. "It has been a little difficult at times, but the more I reflect on the Writing you gave me, the easier it gets. For myself, the change is not so very bad. But I worry about Lenag, and her baby, and my mother."

"It is a sorry thing," Procyon mused. "I wish for the women's sake it were different. But it is good to hear that you are well and adjusting with some ease."

Indi put his arm around the small form of the other man. Even Procyon, he could tell, was feeling the effects of the lean harvest, for he was thin, and Indi could feel individual bones in his back when he should not have. "Where have you been staying?" he asked with a swift pang of worry.

"Oh, away over the hills," Procyon replied, vaguely waving his hand in that direction. "I have even been to Venta, which has seen better days. I haven't been doing too badly myself, honestly I haven't. I have been deeply pondering on the scriptures of Exodus and the Sermon on the Mount."

Indi settled down into the reed floor. "Tell me about them, so."

"Ah." For a moment Procyon's eyes blurred, and he seemed to go away within himself, and when he spoke, it was as though he spoke from far away where things were beautiful and good. "You see, Indi, in Exodus God gave the most memorable part of the law to the children of Israel, and in the Sermon on the Mount, Jesus brought it up again. But in Exodus, he gave the law, the very law that condemned by its sheer weight and our inability to meet its standards—"

"God has very high standards," Indi mused to himself. "He is very perfect."

"Very perfect," murmured Procyon. "And in the Sermon on the Mount, our Lord Jesus revisited these words of God—for they were His very words—upon the hearts of His listeners, and this time He did what He had not done before. The people of his time struggled to obey the *letter* of the law, the form and function of it. But Jesus showed them their deep fault and revealed the *spirit* of the law, that while you do not kill, yet you hate, and that is the same as murder. Though you do not touch, yet you lust, and that is the same as adultery."

Indi shivered involuntarily and shifted again in the pretence of getting more comfortable lest Procyon think his conscience was uneasy. And perhaps it was, he admitted, thinking of Cynr and how much he disliked him. "It-it cut to the heart, did it not?" he asked after a pause. "It made it all even more hopeless than before because—because— " he squinted up his eyes in an effort to remember. "Because the heart is desperately wicked, who can know it?"

"But I, the Lord, search the heart," the little brown man concluded with gravity. "Very good."

Indi flushed with pleasure and hid it in the gathering dark. But then he turned back with as much gravity as Procyon and said, "I have a question, and it is a heavy one."

"Ask on, my son, and I will answer if I can."

Rubbing his nose in the crook of his arm, Indi stared absent-mindedly before himself as the dark came rifling through Thern's fur. He shivered again. "Procyon, what really comes after death? I mean, after the last death. Will all this," he waved his hand around him, "still be here? Will it die, too? What will happen to it when there is no one left to live here?"

"Well, first of all," Procyon replied, "is to remember that the last enemy that will be abolished is death itself. Not defeated—you remember I told you it was defeated when our Lord rose again—but abolished, exiled forever, and lost in the sealed realm of darkness, never to have a hold on us again. As for this earth ... these things too will pass away. When Adam and Eve sinned, all that was perfect was plunged with them into sin as well. Oh, I do not think an irrational creature sins." He fondled Thern's head. "That is for man to do, but they are chained just as we are to death, darkness, and evil. Paul writes that creation groans, awaiting the revelation of the sons of God. It remembers, I think, in dreams, the wonders of the sinless, perfect world. You can hear it in the wild tinkle of the wind through the beech leaves, the splashing of water through cold, crystal streams, the beauty of a hind poised against the sky on a hilltop, and all through heartbreaking, beautiful things that surround us each day. They are memories, dear Indi, memories of long-lost days when God walked with man and all was well, when the lion lay down at peace with the lamb, when the wolf and pony ran together on the heights and laughed at the joke the mockingbird made.

"But all these beauties we see are but dreams in the night, whispers of a hope to come beyond the end of this Age, that wonderful Other Thing. That is what all this is really about, Indi." Procyon's voice, which was all Indi could discern of the man now save the warmth beside him, grew to a glorious crescendo of excitement. "All that has been going on in the vastness of the world—and it is vast, Indi, believe me—is the struggle to reach the perfection of creation, and one day we will reach it! God will not settle for imperfection, but He works in His own ways in His own time. One day He will look down upon the close of this time and the opening of the other and say, 'It is *very* good.' That is what we are living for, that is what stirs our sweet dreams each night, both us and the world, and that is what keeps us going through the dark: knowing that a morning is coming. And while we love the beauty of our world, we must remember that it is only a type, a shadow thing, very faintly resembling what is to come."

Indi reached out and touched the reed nearest him, feeling it carefully along its sharp edge, listening to the way the cold wind whistled in and out of it. "A shadow thing," he murmured. It was all he could do to grasp the meaning of the words and to understand that even the most beautiful and perfect thing he could imagine was only a shadow of its real thing, as a candle is to the full noon-glory of a summer sun, and that real thing he was longing for most. It struck a powerful feeling deep inside him, like a bell tolling for some occasion that he did not know, and he felt a pain unlike any other pain. The taste of the future just eluded him, and in agony he reached for it, longing for that morning to come break up the ragged smoky darkness of his night.

"You cannot have it now," Procyon whispered. "But I understand. My heart, too, longs for it. Sometimes so strongly that I sit down and cry."

Indi looked at his friend. His eyes were shining, for the moon had come up above the trees. "I do not know how to cry," he whispered back. "But sometimes I almost wish I did."

"It is no bad thing to cry," Procyon assured him. "Even our Christos wept." He shifted suddenly and eyed the moon. Voice changing, he said briskly, "You must go back now. Do not expect me often, but I will send Thern to the cattle pond again some time. Now, go quickly."

Indi kissed Procyon's cheeks, rose, patted Thern's wolfish head, and fled back the way he had come through the night. He forgot the basket and the brushwood, but his heart was so much on fire that not all Cynr's wrath could quench it. He watched the moon and said to it, "One day your light will be even more precious than silver." And to the velvet rolling hills, he said, "One day your grasses will sing aloud and sparkle with stars."

In such spirits, he made his way back to the dun.

Slave Wife

Cynr was in a volatile mood. Indi along with Llyeln—who had come up to the houseplace on some pretence of hanging about the Chieftain, as a retainer would—watched warily as the Chieftain whistled and watched the eastward road intently, rocking back and forth on his heels. Every now and then he began snapping a beat with his fingers before he broke off and began pacing, muttering something under his breath. Indi did not feel inclined to ask what was in the wind, for a slave did not speak, but he could not deny the chill of foreboding that he felt had nothing to do with the winter weather.

Suddenly, without warning, Cynr jumped as if stung and said, "Ah!" and walked off down the steps toward the main gate.

"What is it?" Llyeln asked excitedly, standing on tiptoe to see.

Indi, being the taller of the two, rose and gazed across the land. He squinted and flung one arm over his eyes to see against the cold glare of the sun. "A train," he remarked. "Looks like a trader from Venta."

Llyeln pushed off and went to follow Cynr. Halfway to the stairs, he stopped and glanced back. "Aren't you coming?"

Indi shrugged. "I do not know. I do not much care for traders."

Llyeln must have been around when Cynr sold Moch-co, for a swift look of pain came across his features, as if he realized too late he had said too much. He looked at the Chieftain in the distance then back at Indi. The other could see the division of minds within the younger man, how he knew he ought to follow Cynr as Chieftain but knew and believed beyond a shadow of a doubt that Indi and Indi alone was the true Chieftain. Finally he made up his mind and retreated to Indi's side. Smiling broadly, he looked up at Indi's face. Indi returned the look slowly, cracking a smile then giving a small laugh, feeling a little warm inside.

When the spontaneous laughter had died, Indi shifted backward and remarked, nodding toward the advancing traders' caravan, "I do not like it that Cynr is so pleased with their presence. Something is not right about it, and I can smell an ill wind blowing."

"Mmm ..." Llyeln watched a shivering dandelion breaking off its seed-tufts and scattering them over the steps into the air. "Cold, too," he replied, drawing his thin cloak close. "Neither of which I particularly relish."

Indi sighed. "Come on," he said, throwing his arm across Llyeln's shoulder companionably. "Let us go down. Cynr will have our hides if we are not around when he needs us."

Llyeln remarked heavily, "Cynr will have *your* hide, anyway."

Indi could not help thinking how right his friend was.

Strange how it worked out that way. The merchant was the same from the summer past. But this time Indi's eyes did not glitter in amusement as he watched the Spaniard ride into the dun on his mount and lift his voice for the Chieftain. He watched as the Spaniard's face checked for a heartbeat when he learned Cynr was Chieftain and, flickering deftly through the gathering crowd, the merchant quickly caught Indi's eye. A brow lifted then the Spaniard went back to his trade.

Do I look so much like my father, Indi wondered fleetingly, *that even a stranger recognizes me?*

Llyeln was sniffing eagerly like a hound, as though to catch the scent of the wares. Eyes alight, he remarked under his breath, "He's got *girls!*" and he shouldered through quietly to get a better look. Indi remained where he was, a little apart, watching his master carefully to see if he was needed at all. Other than that, he was absent, in his mind sitting by Procyon's side and listening to the words: *Though you do not touch, yet you lust, and that is the same as adultery.* It made him shiver again, and lowering his eyes, he fell to watching his feet. If Cynr needed him, he could always shout his slave's name.

"He brings girls," a soft, questioning voice said at his elbow. Jumping, Indi saw Lenag standing close to him, her hands round her swollen belly, a confused frown on her face. "I … I do not understand."

Indi sucked in his breath. "They are just slaves, like myself," he assured her.

His sister glared at him for an instant. "Do not you be a fool, Indi," she replied tersely. "I know what they are for; do not try to fool me."

Indi put his arm around her and whispered into her hair, "I'm sorry, Lenag. I didn't want you to worry."

Lenag shook her head. "It doesn't matter. I do not even know why I care." With dignity, swollen though she was like a mare ready to foal, she retraced her steps back up to the houseplace, but before she was gone from sight, Indi heard the inevitable, "Indi! Indi-slave! *Indi!*"

The young man shouldered through the crowd and came to his master's side. Strange how it worked out that way. Indi was taller than Cynr now and looked down into his eyes. But Cynr was unabashed, swinging aside to indicate the girls nearest him. "I intend to get a better stock out of you, Indi," he remarked. "Pick one to be your wife."

Indi's heart leapt into his throat. Disbelief rooted him in his place, and for a moment he could not think clearly. *I am dreaming,* part of his mind said. *I am dreaming, and in a moment I shall wake up.* But he did not wake up, and gradually he had head enough to realize that his master was being kind, in a forceful, perverted sort of way. He was offering a marriage. Worse things could happen. So with Cynr watching him and his heart still stuck in his throat, Indi surveyed the eyes of the girls present. Very few would return his look, and with the ones that would he did not like the expression given him. Finally he settled on one with auburn hair and weary eyes who looked ready to collapse any moment. He pointed her out, and for a moment he thought Cynr was going to strike him.

"Her?" the Chieftain asked sharply. "She'd die giving birth to a field-mouse. I think—"

Indi stepped in closer and looked down with burning eyes at Cynr. The two were almost alone, so intent were their looks for each other.

I haven't forgotten that I am Chieftain, Indi's burning eyes said. *Now, you had better not forget it either.*

Cynr relinquished his objection and nodded. The girl was released from her chain and taken up to the houseplace. As if a little shaken by Indi's glare, Cynr said quietly, "You will be given a place of you own. I do not want squalling slave brats running round my house." Then he dismissed Indi and went on with his bartering.

"Honestly," Llyeln was suddenly nearby, "you're doing her a good service putting her in a nice place like this. Walking all day, sleeping in the open, bound to kill a good girl. Though there is not much left of her, you will do all right."

Indi cracked his smile again. "For all your faults," he remarked in a friendly tone, "you are encouraging." He left Llyeln to wonder what that really meant and went up to find Lenag and figure out what sort of creature he had just been saddled with.

Lenag was standing a little uncertainly by the newcomer, and in the light of the open doorway and the fire, Indi could see the girl was trembling with exhaustion. By way of explanation he said with a helpless gesture toward the little thing, "Cynr bought her out for me; she will be my wife. Now, put her in bed and—and feed her."

Despite the thrall-ring round the girl's neck, Lenag treated her as her own sister. Fussing softly round the girl, she bustled the other into the low straw-covered bed that Indi occupied at night. Folding his arms across his naked chest, Indi watched in silence, his questions all unanswered. Would he find his wife as difficult to live with as Lenag found her husband? If only—happy thought—if only he might find her as one of his people! With a sigh, Indi squatted down, cocking an eyebrow and narrowing an eye.

"What is her name?" Lenag asked suddenly over her shoulder.

Indi shrugged. "I don't know. I just know that she would have died if she walked much longer."

They found out later that her name was Sillvia, and Llyeln informed them decidedly that she was of Roman stock. She was small, with olive-tinted skin and that ruddy-auburn expression in her hair. As time passed and she got a little better, her eyes were not quite so weary. But they retained the detached look of a slave that nothing short of death could take away. Indi felt something in his heart twist, and in desperation he wanted to reach out and comfort her, but to what purpose? She was bound to marry a slave and become a slave yet again, to give birth to slaves who would do likewise. As far as she could see, there was no hope and nothing to hold on to. Indi waited in silence for Cynr's bidding, and when Sillvia was strong enough, he and she bound hands and were married, and Cynr gave them a small two-room apartment close by the Chieftain's houseplace.

It was a curious arrangement. Indi felt like a stranger even in his own place, for Sillvia was silent, as if she were mute. She cooked for him, washed for him, and did all the tasks expected of a wife … and a slave. Indi winced one evening shortly after their marriage when he came in out of the flurrying cold to find her waiting to serve him and seeing that she served him as a slave serves her master. He watched as she rose from her side of the fire and beckoned to his food, all in silence. Bowing, she turned and padded away before Indi could get a good look at her face.

He came in and sat, crossing his legs under himself with a groan. Quietly he ate his food. Once he remarked to the shadows, "It is a good meal. Thank you."

The shadows did not reply. Indi lowered his head and whispered into the empty earthen bowl, "God, why doesn't she answer me? Perhaps she is only in shock at finding herself married to a complete stranger and in a completely strange place." He put aside the empty bowl. "I will give her time."

So he did, and in the interim Cynr found plenty of things for him to do, for he was still a slave. "Indi!" he snapped his fingers.

Indi got up from where he had been sitting by his master's hearth among the hounds and came over, crouching on his heels. "Yes?"

"Take my spear down to the smith and replace the tip. I dulled it beyond repair last deer-hunt and I need another for the next season I go out. And pick up my boar-pelt from Fyryrn on your way back. Ah, winter is coming!"

Indi shivered as a gust of wind whipped into the building. The boar-pelt—a magnificent one—would be a good cover for the open door since the old skin had long been too worn and had holes in places where the hungry dogs had gnawed at it. Setting his palm to his forehead, Indi replied, "Yes, sir."

Cynr stopped him suddenly, sticking out his foot between his thrall's legs to halt his progress. Eyeing the shimmering collar about Indi's neck, he asked, "How does it fit you, this new life as my slave?"

Indi shrugged carefully. "I get on," he replied laconically.

Cynr lifted a brow and watched himself wiggle his toe. "I guess only the gods would have guessed that the two best blood-brothers of the dun would become Chieftain and Chieftain's slave. Fate, as the Red-Crests say, threw a strange toss."

"Not fate," Indi assured him; "at least, not the fate you know. As for brothers ..." He thought for a moment, then lifted his head proudly. "I have a better blood-brother now."

For an instant fury lashed across Cynr's face. He was thinking of Procyon, but then he realized, from the old tales of the Brown Man, who exactly Indi was speaking of. He fell back with a rough laugh and waved his hand. "Gods do not bleed, Indi," he said, "no matter what the stories say. A god would never have a mortal for a brother. Now get on with you." He threw a scrap at him, as if he had been a real hound. And the real hounds scrabbled at Indi until he had to shove them all aside to make any headway. At last he got free and was out in the open again in the chilly afternoon wind.

And winter was coming. The wind caught at his scarlet cloak and blew it into a snapping rage at his back as he stepped out onto the porch before the houseplace. The Downs were taking on the hollow-ribbed, white-powdered look they had under frost. The ponies' bony sides were covered in their thick winter mantle of hair, and the children were bound up in their skirts of sheep's hide and woollen tunics.

A firecrest took off from the dry stone wall that held the hill back from sliding into the valley, and following its flight, he saw Sillvia come out of their house and walk quietly down the path to fetch some water. Indi ignored for the moment Cynr's command and went down to her side. She hardly knew he was there, he tread so quietly, and when he reached to take the earthen vessel from her, she started.

"Forgive me, I did not mean to startle you, little one," he said gently.

Sillvia eyed him warily out of the untamed mass of her auburn mane. He had, to this moment, never touched her but at their wedding, had not slept with her or seen much of her on the near side of the fire they shared. So it was strange to be so close to her now, and even he felt odd.

"It is a cold day," he said, offering some sort of conversation to her.

At first he did not think she would answer. She stood rigid, head bowed, her eyes fixedly on him as if expecting him to come round and strike her at any moment. He kept an eye on her likewise while he lowered the bucket into the well. But then she murmured, as though it were hard to get out of her throat, a little, "Yes, lord," and fell silent again.

The rope squeaked and hissed in its pulley. He wanted to think of more to say, but nothing came. She seemed entirely closed to him; even the hair falling over her face seemed like a veil between him and her. So with a wrench of frustration with himself he hauled up the full bucket, emptied it into her vessel, and stood feeling oddly exposed as she took it and went back up the hill to the house without a word. And it came to him in the desolation of her figure that she was lovely, especially the way the wind caught at her mane and made it flare like burnt copper around her neck, but she was a hollow, broken sort of beauty. He longed to reach out and heal her but knew only God could rid her of that terrible expression of pain and loss.

He went on and got the boar-skin from Fyryrn and replaced the spear-tip for his master before heading up the hill again. In the distance he heard a dog barking and thought maybe it was Thern, but having looked, his heart was only disappointed. It had been some time since he had heard from Procyon. He sighed; he would have to do with the words he could remember. They seemed to grow brighter and brighter each time he looked at them in his mind. They kept him going, they and the brief talks he had with Lenag. They were dear to him.

Another Ill Wind

THE WINTER STORMS SET IN quickly after that. Snow came whipping across the Downs, bleak and white and unrelenting. The ponies hated the biting cold, as did the half starved dun-people. The harvest was dreadfully lean and Indi knew, as he stood wrapped in a bearskin cloak in the doorway of his father's house, that the dun was not going to come out of this winter without scars to show for it. He knew people would die, stock would perish, the faces of the survivors grow gaunt and grey. He looked up at the carving of Tir with its slash mark through it. "He has let you do this to us," the young man breathed deeply. "He has given you dominion over this people, but it is I you hate most … because you can't have me."

And that simple thought was cheering. Indi turned from the doorway and came back into the firelight, a half smile on his face as he sank down among the dogs round the blaze. Lenag was seated on a low stool, her belly so round it looked fit to burst. Indi eyed her with concern, much as if the baby were his own because she was his own sister. He glanced at Cynr, who seemed indifferent to the child's pending birth. Indi knew his sister would get little sympathy from that quarter. But Indi also knew that if he took measures to offer his help to Lenag when it came time for the baby to be born, Cynr would come down on him like thunder from the heavens and God alone knew what he might do to Lenag herself. So he had to be content to sit and leave Lenag in God's hands, praying the baby would come safely.

"Indi-slave, you looked pleased with the day," Cynr said accusingly. Indi looked aside at him, and he smiled. "Sing a song then."

The other warriors who grouped about the fire flung up their heads and laughed a little among themselves. Llyeln, crouched across from Indi, frowned. The young slave drew up and twitched his mouth to one side as he thought. "My master ought to ask after Dser, then, if he wants a song, is my thinking."

"You are my slave and have no right to argue, is my thinking," Cynr replied. He settled into his chair. "Sing for me."

Remember David, how he sang for the King Saul? You and he are so much alike, Indi, so sing for him, and pray he enjoys the song. The young man nodded and lifted himself up a little, in the way of good singers, to get room to breathe. The young men leaned forward to see what song Indi map Matheorex would make.

He knew no song specifically, but like the rest he was quick with a tune and swiftly made a song of his own.

"Though he slay me, yet I will praise him," he began softly, his voice a little tremulous at first. "I will rise up in the morning with the dew and praise his name. He has given me a place to serve him, a name with which to be known. He has called me forth and made my heart race with the wind on the Downs, made me soar with the blackbird in the evening. So though he slay me, yet I will praise him. Though sorrows be my lot, yet I will sing. When my last tear has fallen I will take up my song again, I will praise his most glorious, exalted name."

It was clear Cynr disliked the words of the song, but it was also clear that their deep meaning went uncomprehended by him. The tune was beautiful, sung in the rich, husky voice of the young Downland warrior seated before the warm fire with the music of the wind at his back. As each word dropped into the soft shadows Indi's face had grown more serene and sure, and *that* Cynr did not like.

But Lenag understood. Her beautiful eyes were set on him, wide and glowing with appreciation. She looked ready to cry, but somehow she contained the tears of happiness that were welling inside her. Indi glanced her way and saw the look and was at once glad and upset that he had stirred such longing in her.

Cynr saw her train of eye and, without warning, gave her a strike across the face. "Did you look at Dser that way?" he roared, rising to stand over her.

Indi leapt to his feet, cheeks aflame with anger. *She is my sister!* he railed inside his mind. *I cannot let him do that to her!*

Lenag pulled herself together, tipping her chin up proudly. He had embarrassed her before the young men of the dun, but somehow she kept the heat out of her cheeks. "I am sorry I have displeased you, my lord," she said coldly, turning to walk away, her duties by the fire done.

But Cynr grabbed the hem of her skirt and jerked her back. "I was not finished with you, woman—don't you leave me like that!" He suddenly swayed on his feet, and Indi realized he was drunk. He started forward as Cynr put his arms around Lenag and pressed her closer, kissing her neck. It made Indi's blood blaze to see the way he treated her, and in front of the men! But while she was shamed, afraid, and trembling, she gave Indi a warning glance, shaking her head. He had to keep silent or risk endangering her further.

Cynr left off fondling her and pushed her away, his hand closing over the shimmering necklace Procyon had given her. "What?" he cried. Then he lowered his voice. "How many lovers have you had before I got you, hmm? Two at least? Your brother and your Brown Man?" With a cruel jerk he snapped the thong the beaded sword hung from and hurled the thing into the fire. He gave her another smarting slap when she let out an unstoppable cry at the injustice, and without another word flung himself around and left, throwing a thick rug about his shoulders as he stepped into the blizzard, heading for the Hall.

After a tense silence, the warriors got up and left to join Cynr. Only Llyeln stayed, face a bit white, jumping in when Indi went to catch Lenag as she wilted. "Oh, my back," she groaned, leaning in their arms. "Please, just get me to my bed."

"I can manage," Indi murmured to Llyeln. It was no easy task to get a pained woman at any time from place to place; it was even harder to move Lenag, days from her time to give birth, across the entire house to her room. But Indi hefted Lenag up and with some difficulty got her to her bed and put her in it. Llyeln trailed anxiously. When at last it was done and she had lain down she felt a little better.

"I'm so sorry," Indi murmured. "It was a foolish, foolish thing I did."

"You had no choice," she told him, shaking her head. Her eyes began to droop as she began to drift off wearily. "It will turn out right in the end. God … is like that …" And for a moment she was very still, relaxing into the straw-tick bed. So it made Indi jump when she jolted of a sudden, crying out as if in pain.

"What is it?" he asked sharply, thrusting his arm behind her shoulders to hold her up.

"My water has broken," she said shakily. The freckles on her face stood out stark with fear. "Run and get Mother!"

Arm still around her, Indi turned to Llyeln, snapping his fingers. "Run and get my mother!"

Llyeln darted off in an instant, leaving Indi with Lenag for a few tense moments. Her lips were pursed, her body tense; sweat was already beginning to gather on her brow. "Indi, what if it dies?" she whispered.

"Don't think of that now," he told her harshly. "You're going to need all your strength to fight for this thing. You can do it. You are British, after all."

And presently his mother was there with one of the maids. She did not cast him a glance as she entered but with a gesture made sure he knew to leave.

He joined Llyeln on the porch. One look at the other's face and he knew they were both bracing for the rending screams of childbirth and knew that neither of them could stand the noise. "Cisha and Bandr are needing to be fed," he said lamely, as though Llyeln, to whom the two horses had been given, did not know.

They went down to the stables together and stood in the warmth of the long British-style barn with the mares milling about them, their breath faintly grey in their faces. The black colt thrust in, taking a liking to Llyeln, which warmed Indi.

Llyeln looked up from stroking Bandr's ears. "Sillvia..." he began, awkwardly. "How is she? I do not see her about much."

Indi shook his head. "She is having trouble adjusting. I think she has been a slave too long."

Llyeln was quiet for a while. The horses stamped and shifted, brushing up against each other for warmth. And the younger man, twisting his mouth, said, "I am sorry," and left it at that.

The child came by evening. Working up his courage, Indi went to Lenag's room to see it. The warriors were still in the hall, and all was quiet but for the soft sound of the child whimpering in the chilly air. Lenag was lying in bed, ruffled and damp from sweat, looking very disoriented and strained but managing to smile weakly. The baby lay in the blankets by her side, moving its pitiful limbs about blindly in an effort to crawl back into its warm mother and sleep. Indi broke into a smile. "It is well with you, sister?" he asked.

Her voice was very weak and thin, but she murmured, "It is well with me, brother. Come look at her."

Indi stepped across and leaned over the babe. His mother stiffened, almost reaching out to stop him from picking it up, but he shifted his shoulders back a fraction: a gesture of power and command which even she could not deny. So he stooped and lifted the tiny living being in his big hands. How perfect its little body was! Faintly blue, as though made of shadowed marble, rounded, puckering softly, each finger and toe like tiny petals. The eyes were closed, the mouth only a small flower seeking a sun. Tiny and alive! The wonder of it sent a shiver down his spine. He pressed the body against his warm bearskin cloak, blocking out the cold draught. The child stopped whimpering as he ran his warm fingers up and down its back. And Indi realized then that the blessing was upon Lenag and the curse upon Cynr, for Lenag had a beautiful daughter to follow after her, but Cynr had no son to bear his name. Indi felt a slight twinge of pity, but his heart was for his sister and he was glad for her.

His mother gave him a cloth to wrap the baby in. With careful movements he twined the cloth around the body, murmuring in his throat as he did so. "It is small," he remarked. "That is good—it is your first."

Suddenly Indi was aware of another presence, and for one unreasoning moment he shied, thinking Tir was among them. But it was Cynr who stood in the doorway, his deep, dark, smouldering eyes burning through him. He seemed to think Indi was about to devour the baby whole. To avoid conflict, Indi carefully held the child out, breathing heavily, praying hard Cynr would not hurt it.

Cynr took it and looked at it from head to toe, the smoulder never going out of his eyes. Everyone in the room held their breath, even Tirna Mother. Then Cynr lifted his eyes and looked at his wife scornfully. He did not need to say anything; his face said it all. He put the child down on the floor and walked away.

Indi caught up the child and quickly placed it in Lenag's arms. She was crying, her hands over her face. "I did not mean to," she sobbed. "It is not my fault."

"Of course it is not your fault," Indi hushed her. "The girl is as beautiful and precious as any boy could have been. God knit it together, sister; it is wonderful."

She hugged the baby to her chest and sniffed. "It is the one thing on earth I really own," she said softly. "And I love it so dearly."

They heard Cynr's voice from the hall, deep and booming through the house. "Half made it, woman; you only half made it. You would do well to remember that."

Indi had to give Lenag a reassuring glance before stepping outside the room to face Cynr. He was standing at the near end of the fire, arms folded over his chest. Indi went up beside him, harkening back to those days when they had been blood-brothers and dear friends.

"Cynr—master—she has had a long hard labour; you have no right to upset her."

Cynr raised a brow in daring. "You would speak thus to your master?"

"I would speak thus on behalf of my sister."

The Chieftain looked at him, raking him up and down the way he had done the baby. "A slave has no family," he said coldly. "Even you—" he nodded toward the door. "I hear you do not get along so well with your own wife."

"I do not beat her or malign her! I *love* her!" Indi blurted out then regretted his emotions. It did no good to parade them in front of Cynr to sneer at and trample as he wanted.

But it was too late. Cynr began to laugh in a harsh, horrible sort of way. "What do you know about love?" he asked, narrow-eyed. "It took me a while to get it out of her, but your own wife admitted you had never been in to her." He sneered. "You're too intent on your God."

For a moment Indi's mind was a rage. How did he *dare* to say such a thing—*mean* such a thing—about the Lord? But he had to collect himself. *He knows nothing of God; he hates everything of God. Even his own god. What a miserable man.* He held his peace.

"I find the snowstorm better company than you," the Chieftain remarked suddenly, walking to the doorway. He pushed back the flap and ducked out into the blowing white but not before turning and giving Indi a dirty smile.

Black Wolf, Black Smoke

THE WINTER PASSED. IT WAS like the narrowing of a bottleneck: painful to the last moment, straining to an inch of every life in the dun. Many a life was lost, the stock was woefully thinned, and the atmosphere of the place was so heavy Indi felt it would take the power of God to lift it off the ground again. But spring was at last in the air, trembling and uncertain as it was, and winter aconite was peeking through the earth. The first child to spot it sent up a weak cry of discovery, and then came the wail of women praising Tir. Indi went to the door of the houseplace and looked out solemnly.

Dser the bard was dead now, the winter famine having taken him almost at once. His boy had been lonesome without him, and in a desperate dash one night ran off through the cold, only to be found days later in a ditch by the old Legion's Way, quite dead and covered with frost. They had been the first. Others had followed, but to Indi's relief Lenag had grown stronger, as had her daughter. She was named Zeriah-rapha, the healing spice, her name patched together from things Procyon had told them; and it was altogether a foreign name, hung with skin-dark, sunshine mystery.

The child was healthy and full of delight. Indi had become to Zeriah-rapha the father she lacked in the unconcerned Cynr. He was the light piercing through the Chieftain's bitter darkness. Many a day Indi spent frolicking among the rushes with the tiny child, who had learned now to crawl a bit. Before he had been loath to play with children and would certainly not have been found playing with a girl. But now his heart was open to the love

God had poured out in him, and he took it, turned it, and poured it into the child. She soaked it up like a leaf drinking sunlight, rewarding him with a smile. So not only did Cynr hate the child, he hated Indi all the more for relinquishing his masculine authority, kneeling down, and playing in the dust with a woman-child. It was in all ways unheard of. Even Llyeln had been astonished.

"But—but you're the *Chieftain*," he had objected, then shied and looked around lest anyone heard him. "You can't do that."

Indi had raised his head from Zeriah-rapha's soft hair and looked back with a small frown. "Behold, the Lord called the children unto him and blessed them. They are a dawning, a new thing, a possible promise. They stand outside the gates of eternity, not knowing of it, not knowing which path they will take. I pray *she* will be given the right road."

That had silenced poor confused Llyeln on the matter.

A bit of sun broke through the grey scudding clouds and lit up a patch of Down to the northwest, turning the turf a copper and verdigris colour.

"God, it is you who draw up the dead out of the earth, who clothe the land anew each year. The passing of the seasons are in your hand, of your blessing, and to you I aspire no other praise but all."

"What are you saying, Indi?"

Llyeln had come up beside him. It was still cold and they were both dressed in the thick winter bearskin to keep out the chill.

"I was reflecting on how merciful God is," replied Indi.

By this time Indi had made Llyeln come to understand who he meant by "God"; that he referred to neither Taranis nor Tir, nor any other man-made god he had ever come into contact with.

"What has your God done that is so merciful?" he inquired, poking one eyebrow a trifle higher as he looked over the miserable dun.

Indi nodded at the woods. "The buds are opening. The grass is coming back. Look! A stallion is going for a mare. There is a breath of promise everywhere. God is good."

"Indi!"

The voice broke their reverie, and as if they were on a chain both young men whipped around and came ducking back into the houseplace. Cynr was inside, weak from the effects of the harsh winter. But his eyes were bright and hateful as ever. He sat now in a low-slung chair, warm skins draped across his recovering body. Angered that Indi should see him so, angered that Indi had come out of the winter without being brought by the famine to his knees, his spirit lashed out and struck him.

"Why do you stand there like women staring at the sky?" he asked bitterly.

Indi said, "I was seeing the wonder of God in creation."

Cynr said, "I despair of you!" and he brought his hand down on the arm of his chair. Several hounds jumped at his tone. Then he fell into restless silence, moving and shifting about as if he had a thought underneath him as prickly as a burr. Finally he snapped. "There is to be a hunting tomorrow," he said bitterly. "A hunting in which the Chieftains of several Downland duns and some of the warlords from beyond Venta shall attend. Were I well I would attend. Had I a *son*—," he growled into the soft shadows where his wife knelt with his little daughter in her arms "—I would send him with a retainer to at least bear my name. As it is, I cannot even send a retainer."

Indi understood the quandary. To not go would be a disgrace, to send a retainer dangerous because it was likely he would not return to a nearly-starved dun. As if he had had a vision, he knew what was about to happen.

"So," the Chieftain went on, "I am going to send you." He said no more because he did not want to admit that Indi was the one man he would trust.

"As my lord wills," Indi replied softly, bowing. He did not allow himself a smile—that would be too cruel.

"Take your own spear. You'll need no horse."

Indi raised his brows. It was common knowledge that the other warriors would have horses; he was condemned to running to keep up, perhaps over leagues before they cornered their quarry. In the very act of trusting him, Cynr took away the remotest hope of escape. Shrugging, Indi went to prepare.

Indi went down to his house and stepped in quietly, feeling the welcome warmth of the fire after the brisk cold wind of the outdoors. "Sillvia!" he called, looking round the shadows. "Sillvia?"

She came out of the second room, brushing straw off her tunic. "Yes, lord?" she asked in a detached voice, which was all that she could ever bring herself to say to him out of the tangle of her mane.

Indi gave her his customary, hopeful smile—though after an autumn and a winter of receiving nothing in return, the hopefulness was beginning to fade. "I must have my spear and pack for the morrow. I am to go hunting for Cynr."

For a moment something moved across her face, something beyond the dead veil of her eyes. But then it was gone in an instant, so quickly that he hardly saw it. "Yes, lord," she said dully, and turned away.

Meanwhile Indi hunkered down in front of the fire and contemplated the problem of her coldness. He cared for her deeply, and yet he did not know what to do with her. Certainly he understood the role of a wife in the home; he was no fool, but her coldness was a barrier he could not breach just by going to her. That would be cruel, and Indi could not be cruel to her. Hers was an illness, it seemed, that was long and incurable. He wondered what she had been before she had become a slave—if she had been a great princess or a wise-woman or something of great importance that becoming a slave had somehow shattered her life. Like the time Zeriah-rapha had gotten one little paw in the embers of the fire and he had cradled her and soothed her burnt fingers, Indi wanted to cradle Sillvia and soothe her hurts and tell her all was well.

But he knew all was *not* well. Inside the woman was the same darkness that consumed Cynr, the same that had once consumed himself. He knew only one Person could take it away and clean out all the vast void, filling it with peace, light, pleasure, immeasurable trust, and strength. He prayed daily for her soul, going out among the cold, dead fields—as if he were walking through Sillvia's very heart—and falling to the earth in mournful petition. But each time he rose with more peace inside his own heart and came home to find more distance between himself and Sillvia.

Is it to always be this way, my Father? he wondered. *That I am to lose the world—which, you understand, I do not mind so much—but also my wife? Was I wrong in the choice I made? Is this all an irreversible mistake?*

Sillvia brought the spear and pack.

The following morning was chilly and damp with mists. Indi stepped out of his house like a ghost and went down through the dun to the court before the gate, waiting for the shuffle of ponies' hooves in the dark. The sun had hardly come up yet. The hounds were straining at their leashes, snapping half irritably, half excitedly at each other's muzzles. Being a slave, even Cynr's slave, Indi was resigned to the last place in the pack, stumbling often over the milling hounds. But soon the wind was kicking up, high over the mists, blowing up more mists like waves crashing silently and endlessly over more and more waves, and the spirit of the hunt began to take the young man. His legs tensed to feel the smooth Downland grasses hiss by them, and his nostrils flared to take in the scent of the pine. It would be good to be off again, to be running with the pack, to be almost free.

In a short time the hounds got a scent and began to yowl at each other in a kind of argument. The riders urged them after the scent, but almost instantly it was lost again. Another hour was spent finding a new scent. In the meantime Indi got a chance to observe the other hunters. Most of them glanced his way, saw he was a slave, and looked off again. But there was one that looked, hesitated, then found a lull in the hunting to speak.

"You ... you must be the nearby Chieftain's slave," he said, halfway between a remark and a question.

Indi straightened from feeling a broken bush. "I am, lord." It seemed then that the talk would have been over before it was altogether begun, but he became bold and asked, "Are you a Chieftain? And if so, from where?"

But the other man hauled in his pony and avoided a reckless hound. Though older than Indi, he had a light of youth in his eye; he wore a bright scarlet cloak, somewhat worn and aged, and across his shoulders lay a rakish mantle of tabby marten fur. And he saw, with the eye of one trained among horses, that the man handled his tall mare with only one hand; the other arm had only a stump. "Nay," the man said idly, "I am not a Chieftain. I am come from Yr Widdfa valley."

Indi shook his head. "The name seems to come vaguely ... perhaps I heard it from a trader once."

The man took his eyes off the hounds and men who were looking in among the denser bracken before them. "Slave," he remarked suddenly, "your tone bespeaks of breeding. What were you before you were made to wear the thrall-ring? And the thrall-ring—it is a Saxon thing, is it not?" Here he looked sidewise rather sharply.

"I am no Saxon; I am British," Indi said, a frown coming between his brows. He wondered how much to tell this stranger from a western land. But he was lonely, and the man would be gone again soon, so it could not hurt. "Last autumn I was the son of this dun's Chieftain."

"Then how come you to be his slave? What have you done?"

The man spoke in a calm way but also with a hint of surprise and curiosity.

Indi made a cast-away gesture with one hand. "What is there to tell? My brother-in-law took the Chieftainship when I took up the cross of the Christos, and now he and I are ever at odds." As he spoke levelly, almost dully, he kept an eye on the hunting. They had begun to move on again, the hounds crisscrossing over the scent to get the boundaries and direction of the prey.

The man sighed, leaning down in the saddle to nurse a weary knee. "That is an ill thing, slave, though not that you bear the cross of the Christos. *That* is a good thing to hear among these heathen."

"In truth, it is a lonely position," admitted Indi, warming to this warrior. "But I get along. I am not entirely alone."

"That is even better to hear," said the stranger in a far-off, musing tone. And then, "Hail! The hunt is up again!" and they were off at once, streaking through the forest and open glades, and Indi had no more chance to speak with the warrior.

Presently they spied the quarry. It had paused a moment on an outcropping of rock in a meadow, looking back, and his heart lurched to see it: it was a handsome, powerful black wolf. And almost as soon as the young man took this in he was breaking through the pack of hounds and horses, almost ignorant of what his legs did, and was flying across the ground of thick oak-scrub and lichened rock flecked like shorn salmon with the others shouting after him not to be a fool. The wolf whirled on the rock and shot into the wood, but he was after it, spear in hand, well choked and poised for action. It was not vengeance that spurred him on or the sense that he was about to slay a god. It was that, for the first time in a long, long time, this was *his* kill, and he relished it. Not for the wanton joy of killing—this wolf would prove dangerous to the herd and must be killed anyway—but for the thrill of the master of animals to hold in his hand the power over life and death, and to choose death.

Indi sped across the glade, his feet a whirl beneath him. The shouting dwindled and faded away into the background of his mind. He tumbled headlong down a slope, leapt a burn, and rushed up a gravely cliff, the flicker of black always before him. Through the ragged pines he ran, almost bent double on the slope, and he flung himself without a thought to his own hide after that flicker of black into the mouth of a cave.

The darkness welled up at him like a barrow's inside, full of the sound of his breathing and the wolf's snarling. It turned at bay and lunged at him, but the fury of the fight was upon him. He ducked to one side and rammed his spear into the animal. It howled and clashed its jaws around his ears, but he would not be shaken off. He retracted the spear and plunged again, only this time he missed and gouged a hole in the cave wall. He fought off the wolf with his heels until he regained his posture and had space to thrust again. This time the spear went cleanly through the skull, ripping open the mess of brains all up the shaft.

Indi got the spear out and dragged the still body into the open to get a good look at it. Scornful and disappointed, the other hunters were milling around the base of the cave—disappointed, but not brave enough to plunge in with him and face a wolf in the dark. The strange warrior, however, was halfway up the slope when Indi came out bloodied from head to toe, and hailed him.

"Light of heaven!" he exclaimed when he got a look at Indi. "Have you—well, that was finely done!"

Indi straightened, glowing with the praise. He slung his prize across his shoulders, politely declining the stranger's suggestion that he carry it on pony-back. They made their way back to the dun, arriving at the close of twilight. Supper was laid out for them in the Hall. Indi joined them, having washed and redressed.

A depressing sentence awaited him. Cynr was seated on his throne, though ill and a little lopsided, and eyed him intently as he came through the door. It was the look of severe displeasure which brought either the whip of reality or the whip of words. Tonight it was a bit of both.

"I hear you killed the wolf today, Indi-slave," he snapped.

Indi nodded. "Indeed, sir, I did. I hope my master is pleased with the skin I brought him."

Cynr laughed harshly. "It is forbidden of any in this dun to slay a black wolf! Did not Angog make that clear after the black wolf attacked you? Did he not burn the body of the wolf in ceremony to Karmer? And—" here he rose slightly in his chair—"*are we not to burn this one?*"

Indi stood his ground beneath the oppressive glare of his Chieftain. He had heard no such mandate from the priest, though he would have wisely obeyed it just to keep peace if he had. But the deed having been done, he knew there was nothing wrong in killing a black wolf.

Cynr leaned forward and brought his hand smartly across Indi's face. "I have half a mind to give *you* to Angog, you disobedient whelp!"

At that moment the stranger got up and came over hesitantly but with dignity. Cynr looked his way with surprise. "Sir," the man said quietly.

"You wish to speak with me?" Cynr asked, waving Indi back.

"Yes, sir," said the stranger, glancing at Indi. "I wished to ask a trade with you. I would like to buy your slave."

Despite the sparks of pain in his eyes from the blow, Indi's heart suddenly shot sky-high. He felt intoxicated, light-headed, dizzy with the thought. Here was a man he would serve with his whole heart! Here was a man who would not beat him and mistreat him for his belief in God. He held his breath.

Repositioned in his seat, Cynr leaned forward and clasped his thin hands on the sides of his chair, staring intently into the stranger's face. Suddenly he broke the silence with a howling laugh. "You want to buy *him*? That slave is both a curse and a blessing in one body. He brings down the wrath of the gods upon us, and yet he serves me as if he were some dumb, witless hound."

"I perceive otherwise, sir," replied the stranger. A frown darted like the shadow of a swallow over his face. "He is neither dumb nor witless, and I cannot imagine that the gods would have any power over him. I would buy him."

"Well, you shan't, at any rate," was the reply.

Indi's heart hit a deeper depression than any he had ever known. Without thinking he turned and left the hall. He collapsed just outside the door, all his strength sucked out of him, huddled in the cool dark of the night. The songs that were being struck up inside grated on his nerves. The smoke seemed stuck in his brain and made it painful to think. He sat for a long time, staring at the stars and trying to ask why, *why* had he not been able to go with the stranger?

After a long time the stranger stepped out into the dark, almost passed him, then stopped as he recognized the figure in the shadows. "I am sorry," he whispered, setting a hand to Indi's shoulder. "I fought for you."

"It does not matter," Indi rasped. "I have a wife here anyway."

The stranger took this in for a moment, considering the stars as Indi had done. "Well," he breathed, still looking at the sky with the wind kicking up the fur of his marten mantle, "if you can contrive to gain your freedom," he looked down, "search for me—Lord Bedwyr—in Yr Widdfa. If I am not there, if my lord's party has moved on, look for me among the Dumnonii, on the western coast where the land falls into the sea. I should be there if our God has not taken my life before then."

He began to move off through the dark, but once again he paused and looked back. Indi was unable to see any features of his face, but he would always remember him afterward: not very tall but tall enough, a trifle bow-legged from lots of riding, very Roman in a queer, British sort of way, full of patience that stemmed from the knowledge of horses and—most importantly—God. "You may be coming westward, at any rate," he said. "Some of the men are speaking of Woodhenge."

"I know nothing of the place or name," Indi replied bitterly, curling up tighter. Like a sick hound he wanted chiefly to be left alone to lick his wounds in quiet.

Lord Bedwyr rubbed his palm across the back of his neck and stiffened as a chill wind kicked up stronger against them. "It is a pagan circle northwest of here, made of wood—a great big enclosure. Your priest seems interested though your Chieftain seems dubious."

Indi shrugged. "It does not matter to me."

The lord from Yr Widdfa merely shrugged in answer and walked off to his bed. Indi did not see him again until the party was leaving the following morning. It was a clear day, and the trees in the forest were beginning to put forth their springtime show. Indi stood by the door of his house and looked down on the cavalcade, but lifting his eyes, he looked up and saw a column of black smoke rising with the dawn over the treetops.

Angog was burning the wolf.

Woman Trouble

It was hot August when Indi next heard from Procyon. The fields were thick with the harvest, a far better harvest than the previous year, though it was not yet ready to be brought in. He was weeding in a patch not far from the forest when he heard a distant whine and looked round, snatching up his spear. He thought at first that the animal peering at him from behind a bush was a wolf—it was certainly brindled and shaped like a wolf—but it got up and took a step closer then sat down again, wagging its tail at him. With a rush of joy Indi looked round hastily to be sure no one was watching him then slunk off through the forest to meet Thern.

It was a wonderful reunion. He struggled with the dog over the crackling old leaves, digging his hands into the deep rough fur, smelling the old greasy smells. They were both laughing, but then Thern got up and looked at him as if to say, "We mustn't keep Procyon waiting."

"No, of course not," Indi replied without bothering to think he was talking to a dog. But they were running now through the forest, headed for the river. Something hard and painful twisted beneath his breastbone when at last he broke through the shrivelled bracken and saw the little brown man hunched over the water.

"Procyon!" he called in as loud a voice as he dared.

Procyon swung around and saw him, breaking into a wide grin. "My boy!" he cried, taking Indi into his arms. They embraced until they could hardly breathe then backed away to look at each other.

"You are thinner," Indi remarked, frowning accusingly.

"And you are bigger." Procyon struck his shoulder proudly. "How has the famine been?"

Indi sat down and stretched out his legs, running his hand over the back of his neck. "Rough," he answered. "But the crop is promising this year. I pray it will go well with the dun."

Procyon nodded. "I've felt the famine a bit too, but not so much north where I've been."

Indi's head came round as he looked intently at his friend. The despair came back, along with the intense longing to be free. But he pushed it aside. "Procyon," he said, "have you heard of Yr Widdfa?"

The other frowned at him. "Yes," he said slowly. "A great warlord lives there, when he is not busy putting out fires on the rest of this island."

"Do you know where it is?"

Procyon's frown deepened. "Indi," he admonished sternly, "you are not contemplating escape, are you? Remember God has set in motion the powers over you for you to obey so long as you do not break the meta-law of God himself."

"I had no such intention," assured Indi, "though in my heart I often wish for a space to breathe the night air as if I were a freeman. But no, I was thinking about you."

"About me?" Procyon was perplexed.

Suddenly a crack made them both turn round and look with pale faces. Llyeln had come through the brush, holding Indi's spear, which he did not remember dropping. When the young man caught sight of the Brown Man he froze as if moonstruck, eyes huge in his head.

Indi scrambled up. "Do not say a word of this, Llyeln!" he commanded in a low, urgent tone.

"I do not think he meant to spy on us, Indi," said Procyon, regaining his composure.

But Llyeln took a step forward, confused and frightened. "What is he doing here?" he asked Indi sharply. "He cannot stay; he *must* go—for your sake, Indi! They will—" he glanced over his shoulder. "They will kill him."

"I always knew you had a gentle heart; God bless you," murmured Procyon.

Indi looked from friend to friend, measuring the difference between the two. But Llyeln was right. He set his hands on the little brown man's shoulders and embraced him. "It has been too short," he whispered, his throat taut. "But you must go. Go to Yr Widdfa," he admonished suddenly. "Go and ask after a Lord Bedwyr. Tell him to remember a young slave he once fought for—he will understand. Nay, do not ask questions. For once think of me as the Chieftain I should have been and obey me."

Procyon took this in quietly. "Yes," he replied with gravity. "I see you are right. I take it you wish to see me again?"

"If I can contrive to gain my freedom, I will meet you in Yr Widdfa. If Lord Bedwyr is not there, search for him among the Dumnonii, on the western coast where the land falls into the sea. You will find him there, he told me."

The little brown man gave him another embrace. Then he whistled up Thern and disappeared as he always disappeared into the bracken down the riverside, drifting back out of Indi's life.

With a heavy sigh and a heavy heart Indi turned to Llyeln. "What brings you here?" he asked quietly.

Llyeln hung his head like a whipped dog. "I meant no harm. I did not mean to barge in on your talk. Forgive me."

Indi put a hand on the younger man's shoulder. "You did nothing wrong, I suppose. I am jealous of that man's company. He is the greatest man I ever met. But you are pale! Are you ill?" He bent to get a good look at Llyeln's face.

Llyeln blushed then paled again to the colour of dead ashes. He seemed about to be sick. "I'm not … not ill," he started.

"You are ill," Indi insisted. "Is it the heat?"

"I am not."

"Then what is it? Is Lenag ill? Has Cynr done something to her?" Indi's heart suddenly began to race.

"No, she's well. Cynr hasn't done anything to her that I know of…"

Frustrated, Indi insisted, "You *are* ill, Llyeln—"

The young man flared, "I am not!" Then, swallowing back, he said, "There has been some trouble, Indi."

He stared back at Llyeln, counting out the time with his heartbeat. His stomach slowly clenched and unclenched. The taste of fear began to gather at the back of his mouth.

"It's—woman trouble."

His stomach clenched.

"It's yours."

The clenching forced the taste of fear into the front of his mouth, and it was all he could do to hold it back. A new sort of pain was thrusting itself up under his breastbone, and he remembered afterward thinking very clearly, *Why do you do this to me, why this after I was so happy?* Then he found himself turning on his heel toward the dun, treading heavily through the bracken, aware of Llyeln trailing silently in his wake.

"Who was it?" he asked suddenly, as though it mattered. "It was not Cynr, was it?"

"No," Llyeln assured him. "It was an outdweller. He's been caught."

"Does anyone know of this?"

Again Llyeln shook his head. "No, only you and I and Cynr."

Indi broke the cover of the forest and began to ascend the hill to the dun, all the while his mind a raging torrent of feelings. His mind was numb with shock, the centre of his chest throbbing, and he felt as though he had swallowed watered ash. And yet at the same time it was as though he were walking through a dream, some wretched nightmare that kept his belly clenching in disbelief, a dream he would surely wake up from in a moment. But he did not wake. His feet kept walking somehow, his belly kept clenching.

Llyeln had to run to keep up. "Indi!" he cried. "What are you going to do?"

The question brought him back out of the feeling of surrealism. For a while Indi was unable to answer. He had to decide himself. "I am—I am going to talk to her," he heard himself saying thickly round the sickness in his middle.

The other was incredulous. "But Indi, she slept with an outdweller! A nobody! You can't just—"

"Can't I?" Indi asked sharply, spinning round. And suddenly things seemed very clear. "She is my wife, Llyeln." He stopped then to look at the clearness of the thing and to think about what he had just said. He felt much the same way as when he had told Cynr he loved her: it did no good to parade his feelings; but the very words that had come out of his mouth seemed, in some confused way, to be a comfort and a truth he could cling to.

Llyeln was subdued, his whole body straining in shame away from Indi. "I am sorry," he whispered.

Indi felt even worse. He laid a hand on his friend's shoulder and squeezed tightly. "I did not mean to lash out at you, friend." He emphasised the last word. "What do *you* think I will do?"

For a while Llyeln was silent, pondering this while watching a small hot wind blow a tuft of seeds down the track. "I think you will forgive her," he remarked at last. "You are that sort of man."

This is why, he thought. *Ruthless is my God's love, to rip away my happiness to make me holy.*

He left Llyeln on the road and went up to his house. It was desolate with an air of resentment that greeted him at the door. How cold the doorposts felt beneath his hands! Stepping down into the room, Indi saw a shaft of sunlight pouring through the firehole, and in the midst of the light crouched a single figure, bent over, white as chalk. Her face was drawn and lifeless. There were even cuts on her body, which redoubled the pain Indi was now feeling like a wave of nauseating smoke washing over him.

Sillvia did not move as Indi walked up to her and stood on the near side of the fire, looking resolutely down at her. Her shingle-grey eyes were wide and fixed. Very deliberately Indi drew his knife and flung it down into the earth between her knees. For a moment the only sounds were its airy whistle, the small thud of its contact, and the sharp intake of startled breath from the woman. Then it was almost unbearably quiet and Indi waited.

After a while Sillvia reached out and grasped the knife with a cold white hand. With a swift movement she set the point to her breast and sucked in another breath. "You want me dead."

"No," Indi replied in a low tone, "it is the other way around. If you were to plunge that knife into *my* heart the pain would be less than what I feel right now. It is not my intention to prick your conscience—only the Lord Almighty can do that. But I wanted you to know." His eyes softened as he gazed at her. With each word the waves of pain became alternately easier and harder to bear. She looked so helpless, so lost, so fragile. He remembered her as he had first seen her, trembling, her loose, heavy auburn locks falling as they did now around her thin, mousy face, and something tightened in his throat.

The knife dropped with the listless hand. "Why do you not kill me? Is it because I am only a slave and not worth the bother? Is it because of the Chieftain?"

"It is because you are my *wife*, and you always will be," replied Indi sternly.

Sillvia turned her head away to hide her angry tears. And all at once Indi was looking at her as if for the first time, beyond the slave train, really seeing the woman and not the silent, stone-cold slave woman he had married by force. "But you were never here," she protested weakly. "Always you are at the Chieftain's house-place, always you fawn for him."

"I am his slave," Indi reminded her, "and I must serve him. But no matter where I go, no matter what I do, this is always home, with you waiting for me beside the hearthfire. And I always pray for you, you know. I always pray God will give you his strength and saving mercy."

Sillvia laughed mockingly. "Obviously your prayers went unheard."

But the laugh was hollow, the mockery weak, and Indi summoned all the faith given him. "But I do not think so. In the Scriptures, the Word of God, the Christos said to one of his disciples, 'Peter, Satan—that is the devil, our enemy—has demanded to sift ye like wheat. But I have prayed for thee. When thou turnst, strengthen thy brethren.' I think this must have happened for this purpose: your salvation."

But she shook her head, her hair falling over her shoulders like a mantle. "Not—not myself," she said. "Not after—"

"No," Indi interjected. "There was a woman who was recorded in the Holy Scriptures as committing adultery as you have done, and she was brought in shame before the Christos for judgement. Indeed, her accusers meant to judge the Christos, to make Him either a murderer or a man bereft of God's law. Their custom then was to hurl stones at the offender until he or she was dead. But the blessed Lord knew all the wicked intents of their hearts and said to the crowd, 'Let he who has no sin cast the first stone.' So all went away but the woman, who sat before the Christos much as you do before me. He rose from inscribing His wisdom in the sand at His feet and inquired of her, 'Where are thy accusers?' and she said, 'All have gone, my Lord.' So the Christos replied in the fullness of His wisdom, 'Neither then shall I accuse thee. Go thee and sin no more.' For He Himself had come as an atonement-offering for sin, to make such as her clean. And so there is pardon, full pardon, from the lips of heaven's justice."

There was a long stretch of silence while Sillvia took this in. Indi himself felt a sort of surprise that he had recounted this story so well, for he had only heard it once in passing. But now it sprang out like a flower after a rain, bright crimson and glorious.

At last Sillvia said rather dejectedly, "I wanted to hurt you. I was very angry with you so that my soul could think of nothing more. But—I know I am as much at fault as *he*—I was truly sick with the whole thing. Honestly, lord, I was." She gazed up at him a moment, her eyes full of sorrow, then, finding herself unable to hold his eyes, she dropped her own to the dirt at his feet. "Only I could not get out," she went on randomly, miserably. "It was like being in a pit that closes you in and all hope out …"

Indi stepped across the hearth, over the dead ashes and the rift between, knelt, and embraced his wife. All his love and pain swelled in his chest until he felt he would rend apart. And she was such a little thing! She folded into his arms easily. But she struggled against him. "No, lord, do not touch me! Please, I am unclean."

"No more unclean than I was," whispered Indi. He searched gently for her face. "You are my wife."

"But I am dirty! Please—"

Indi got a gentle but firm hold on her jaw and forced her mouth against his. The rest of her was cold and dry, but her lips were warm and alive, trembling even, uncertain. Indi felt a burst of life inside him at their touch. She struggled a little, but he pushed her over and lay with his lips questing for hers, his powerful arms holding her fragile body. But after a while, when she had long ago ceased to struggle and had put her own arms around his shoulders contendedly, he rolled onto his side and watched her face. Her lips were still parted and she was breathing a little heavily, but so was he. He put his hand around her slender throat and kissed her again.

Sillvia's eyes had lost the coldness of their shingle-grey and now glowed anew with the soft rays of the sunlight pouring in around them and kindling a glow in her eyes. They turned up and gazed at Indi as she whispered, "Is your God like that?"

Indi chuckled. "Perhaps," he whispered back. "But I think His love is much more fulfilling and fierce than mine."

She drew him back down. "A *loving* God," she murmured in rapture. And as a wind blew in through the smoke-hole of their room, it stirred up a little spark of yellow among the straw, and Indi saw, as it tumbled into Sillvia's splayed auburn hair, that it was a fresh bloom of hawkbit.

Wind in the Wheat Sheaves

Indi found himself leaving his father's hall and going home earlier in the evenings than before. He found his heartbeat quickening a little as he jumped up the steps and ducked into the room with its bloom of fire in the hearth and Sillvia, always by the fire, with her auburn hair burnished gloriously in the light, rising to greet him. At last it was good to go home.

There was a faint chill in the air one evening as he stepped in out of the gathering dark. An elusive scent of autumn was in the air, and with the wind blowing so strongly as to make a sea-surf noise through the wheat-sheaves, he held his cloak around himself a little more tightly than he had before.

Sillvia looked round from the fire, coming up from her knees in one smooth motion. "My lord...! You are a little late. Has Cynr been cross with you?"

He flung off his cloak and wrapped his arms around her as she came to him. "Cross?" he murmured. "I do not remember.... But it is good to be home. It has been a long day."

"So." She dropped her head into the hollow of his shoulder and pulled her arms tight round his ribcage for a moment, and he, holding her, pulled in the scent of her hair and the cakes that were heating on the hearth stones by the fire. "Zeriah-rapha and her mother, how are they?" she asked.

And he remembered that Cynr had been cross and had been arguing with Angog again, which had made the child cry. Cynr had told Lenag to silence the child, and she had done her best, but in the end Indi had stepped in and taken his niece away to the apple garden so that Cynr would not do his sister any mischief.

"They are folding up into bed now, the two of them," he told Sillvia. "The day was long for them, too."

She caught his meaning but said nothing. Breaking away from his grasp, she returned to the fire to finish his supper. He trailed her, unwilling to be far, content to sit and watch her turn and turn about as she stirred the stew and flipped over the cakes. She had caught up her mass of hair into a thong, but the day, which had been long, had pricked out tendrils to fall around her face, and then ends of them seemed to flare like a candle's wick in the light of the fire. Small and lovely and warm, she made for a pleasant image.

There came an unexpected knocking at the doorpost. Sillvia straightened from the hearth; Indi twisted round, brows crunched in surprise.

"Llyeln?" his wife asked.

He got to his feet. "Llyeln would not knock." He crossed the room, feet in the encroaching shadows, and bent to haul back the heavy doorflap, stepping away to let the light of the fire fall across the threshold.

It was not Llyeln. To his compounded surprise, Tadc and Mylor, two of the Cynr's warriors and some of his old companions, stood at his door, their hoods thrown up over their faces so that the firelight barely touched their eyes. There was a quick flurry of panic in his belly, but when they made no move to touch him, he said, "Will you come in?"

He stepped back farther to let the two come slipping in and quickly let the doorflap drop behind them, fastening it to the post before turning to see what the men could want so secretly with him.

They were standing uncertainly near the middle of the room, glancing about like animals in a cage. Sillvia stood looking at them no less warily, her head tipped up, her eyes very bright in her face, which was an expression Indi had never seen in her before.

"A blessing on the guests of this house," she said presently. "And peace to all who enter."

Tadc roused himself to answer. "A blessing on the woman of the house, and peace to all who partake of her bread."

Seemingly satisfied, she knelt back on her side of the fire to keep the cakes from burning, and Indi stepped forward to indicate the food. "It is windy and cold outside tonight. Come eat with me."

Out of courtesy Tadc and Mylor had no choice but to shrug off their cloaks and sit beside him, taking the bowls of stew and cakes that Sillvia served them. For a while they sat and ate in silence. Indi longed to know what brought them, but courtesy forbade him from inquiring until they had either eaten their fill or brought the matter up themselves.

Tadc-Hound had taken up his second cake when he stopped, put it away, and turned to Indi. "Indi map Matheorex," he said, "there is a thing that Mylor and I have come to ask of you."

Indi put away his own bowl. "Ask on," he replied, a little bewildered.

The warrior tucked his hands under his armpits and pulled his shoulders up around his ears, staring into the heart of the fire. The fire flickered on his face, and for a moment he did not seem there, as though he were not looking out of his own eyes. "A year ago," he began, "a year ago now, you had come to draw away from us your trail companions, and we felt the gap keenly. And a year ago, in something that I thought was jest, but now I think was spite, I mocked you for not coming with us. But now it is in my mind that yours was a narrow road to be tread alone, and you had no love for our trail."

Indi listened in silence, watching the way the light leapt and flickered in the other's distant eyes, the way the shadows gathered in the folds of his cloak sprawled across his knee. He was aware of Sillvia watching from across the fire out of the fringes of her lashes.

Suddenly Tadc looked round hard, seeing out of his own eyes once more. "Is it a very narrow road, this trail you are on?" he asked like a knife thrust.

"It is," Indi heard himself saying.

"And … is there no room for others on this trail?" Tadc ventured. "For two, at the very least?"

And he was remembering back a year, a year and over a year, to the dream that his mother had dreamt when the first summer storms had come thundering in, of the little brown voice and how it had sprung up, persistent and beautiful, until it burned a thousand points of silver in the dark. And he said, "Yes, Tadc, there is room. For two, and for two hundred, and for two thousand beside. It is a narrow trail, but a dozen hunters can run single file on the same buck-path."

Tadc stared at him hard for a few moments more, as if to be sure Indi did not remember his mocking, as Llyeln had once said, and throw it back in his face now. But Indi held the fellow's gaze, and finally the other's shoulders unfolded, and he said in a breathless kind of laugh, "Well, then it seems we hunt together, you and I, and Mylor."

"The quarry is holiness, and it is a swift quarry," warned Indi. "Is it a good hunting?"

And Mylor, who had been quiet until now, looked up from where he had been staring into the dark emptiness of his bowl. "I am thinking that the God who put his collar on you and set you to the quarry is not a bad God to be running trail with."

"Then repent," said Indi, "and believe. For long and long He was silent among our people, but He has spoken now, and He has made a way of redemption. He has made Himself the reconciliation between His holiness that He is and the evil that we are. The quarry follows but one trail, and we only live who follow that quarry."

Tadc gathered himself together and rose. Mylor got up silently beside him, nodding to Sillvia. "It is late," Tadc told Indi. "And if Cynr catches us here, it will surely mean ill for you. We will go—for now. Good hunting, brother."

"Good hunting."

Indi followed them to the door and held the flap back for them, the light spilling out between his legs into the emptiness of the lane as the two young men flickered away into the night. He watched them go until they were out of sight, the tips of his fingers cold in the outside air.

"The door, Indi," said Sillvia. "It is chilly tonight."

He looked up at the sky. A gust of wind came down the lane, and he noted with a sense of foreboding that the sky was overcast and there was something in the wind that was not autumn, something that worried him. But Tadc and Mylor pushed the thought out of his mind and he dropped the flap.

Sillvia turned from putting away the last of the bowls from supper. "It is chilly tonight!" she repeated huskily. Worming her way under his arm against his side, she added, "You are so warm...."

"I think that Tadc and Mylor have made me rather warmer," he admitted. "To think—it is almost unbelievable."

As they went into the second room and climbed under the warm striped rugs, Sillvia replied thoughtfully, "But I think that we are all unbelievable."

She drifted off shortly after, and Indi lay in the dark with his arm around her little soft figure, looking up through the darkness at the thoughts in his head. He had friends within the gates now, and he had something to be Chieftain over, after a fashion. The sound of the wind turned to rain overhead and he was hearing the way Mylor had tapped rhythmically on his bowl, which he had not noticed before. And suddenly he jolted into wakefulness out of his thoughts to find the sound was still going on, persistent, rattling, erratic with the rushing of the wind.

At his sudden movement Sillvia groaned and turned over, searching for his warmth. "Indi? What is it?"

"Listen!" he hissed back, and they sat in the dark, heads craned back, listening to the sound. It was the sound of rocks falling onto the thatch, rolling off and banging into each other. He could feel the pound of his heart against his wife's hand on his chest.

"*Hail*," she whispered desolately.

The hail kept coming until daybreak, and it was a dismal day that awaited the dun. The fields were stripped as if the hand of death had raked its claws through and through.

"You will kill us all," Cynr rasped at Indi behind his clenched teeth as they surveyed the wreckage of their crop. "Where is Angog?"

Angog was sent for, and Indi, to keep peace, left Cynr and went walking out into the cold fields alone, feeling a sense of awe and disappointment. Silent and cold, they stared blankly back at him, washed grey and flat like a wall between him and the world beyond the clouds. Indi looked down and around at the desolation. It looked as if a Roman legion had come through, devastated the land, and sown salt on the earth. He did not know if a crop would ever be brought in again from this valley or whether the curse of God truly was upon it.

"Is it because of what they have done to you?"

Indi turned around and saw Sillvia nearby, standing at the edge of the field. She was wrapped in a dull-coloured mantle which the wind was trying its best to tear away from her. Her auburn hair was whipping round her face, her eyes narrowed against the sting of the cold. He went to her quickly and held her to keep her warm. "Why are you out in the cold?" he asked.

"Is it because of what they have done to you?" she repeated.

"I do not understand. What is the 'because'?"

She nodded at the field. "That there is no crop even on the eve of the harvest. Is it so?"

Indi shook his head. "I do not know, my dear; how can I say why God does what He does? But let us be silent and wait on Him. Let us see what our God will do."

It was not until the following morning when the arguments between Cynr and Angog had sputtered out into sullen quiet that Indi felt safe enough to go up to the Chieftain's hall. It was too early for Cynr to be up, the hounds were lying about, and the other servants were still abed and snoring. Indi moved like a shadow among them, fixing a blanket here, lifting a leg back onto a cot there, and finally squatted down to stoke up the fire and bring some warmth to the cold room.

A dog whined softly. Indi turned and saw Lenag with a rug wrapped tightly around her, standing in her bedroom doorway. "Cynr is fast asleep," she sighed. "He drank his sorrow away last night."

Indi's face darkened in a frown. "Are you unhurt?" he asked.

She smiled and nodded her head. "Yes. You and I are Chieftain's children; we are wise. But no, he was too drunk to know me from the shadows last night. And how are you and Sillvia?"

"We are well," he replied, bending to the fire. "We had an unexpected—but I hear the cubling calling. Bring her out and I will tell you."

Lenag fetched the babe and sat to feed her while Indi made up the fire and scratched a hound's head. She waited patiently as Indi sought for the right words. For a while the only sounds were the child and the crackle of the fire. "Two of the warriors," he said finally, shifting to fold his arms across his knees, "came to me last night. It seems that He who has made man's mouth, the deaf, the mute, the seeing, and the blind has worked between the three of us so that I could speak, and they could hear, and the blind were made to see."

Lenag cuddled Zeriah-rapha in her arms, her face overtoned with bliss. "Our God moves and all creation feels the power of it," she whispered, listening to the howling winds. "Oh, Indi, He is being felt in this place!"

"Yes, and this place likes it none too well," he remarked dryly. "I fear the other gods will fight as hard as they may against us. However," he rose and dispelled her glance of fear, "our God is stronger far than they. We take comfort in that. Now, if you are finished with the cubling, Medi will take her out of your hands for a while."

CIRCLE WOOD

THE DEVASTATION OF THE HAIL storm was felt even more heavily than the previous famine. Not a piece of wheat, not a grain, survived the pounding of the storm. Spirits plummeted and Cynr, in an attempt to hold the dun together, made a desperate decision. It was made one horribly sunshiny day when the fields ought to have been bare because of the harvest, not trampled by the angry heavens, and when Indi had already broken up several serious quarrels between the younger warriors because of the prevalent discontent and uncertainty.

Indi was keeping himself busy seeing to Cynr's pony, who had gotten a stone in its frog and was listless for want of grain. He had struggled with the animal for over an hour, coaxing it to eat what little he had to offer. It lipped at his palm and shook its head wearily.

"I know, cousin," Indi sighed, setting his hands on his hips. "We are doing what we can."

There was a flurry of footsteps behind him, and he turned to see Tadc and Llyeln come ducking into the stable. They looked around, spotted him, and came over. He had no time to speak before Llyeln was tumbling the story out. "Cynr and Angog are going at it hammer and tongs, Indi," he said. "There's talk of leaving, leaving the dun altogether. Angog says the place is under a curse, that we will die if we stay here."

Indi glanced at Tadc and saw his own thought run across the other's face at the same moment: *Angog will make us the scapegoats and leave us adrift if there is a leave-taking.* And he was not sure if he liked the idea or not. It was a wide, uncertain world. But he pushed the pony's head away and thrust himself between the two men's shoulders, heading for the Chieftain's hall.

"Where are you going?" asked Llyeln.

"To see Cynr," Indi shouted back. "He needs me."

The air was crackling with uneasiness when he entered. Cynr was seated in his hall with a handful of other warriors around him. Angog was standing in front of him, arms folded, head down in thought. He skirted the priest, hoping not to catch his eye and make more trouble, and squatted down by Cynr's chair.

The Chieftain glanced his way. "Come to add your voice to the matter, have you?" he asked bitingly.

"Voices," said Angog moodily. "Voices and voices, little brown voices. *His* voice," he said, thrusting out a finger at Indi, "like a snake's poison—adder's tongue!—killing so many so quietly. A voice crying in the wilderness, crying over the dead in the wilderness like a hawk crying over carrion. *Kin-slayer*."

Indi flinched at the last accusation, seeing his father's sallow face and vacant eyes. *Kin-slayer.* The part of him that was not a slave welled up at the insult, and if it were not for the sight of Lenag's child playing among the hounds, he might have done something he regretted to Angog.

"Leave him be," Cynr said unexpectedly. "Leave him be, priest. He is kin. And whether he is the curse or not, I will leave you to ask the gods on that score. He serves like a dog and always comes back to the collar. Is it or is it not the will of the gods to go to this Woodhenge? And will we prosper there? My only concern is the dun-people and the horses."

Letting the matter go, Angog said, "The haruspices say nothing of prospering," he admitted. "They indicate that Woodhenge is but a resting place on our road and that we will wander to the west until we come to a temple of stone, and there we will offer up a liberating sacrifice, and the curse will be broken."

Cynr sat with his chin in his hand, staring at the way Indi was idly drumming his fingers on his knee. "You are asking us to go on a pilgrimage?" he said presently. He pulled his head out of his hand and eyed the priest. "I have livestock to care for, to breed and break. I have people to feed. We cannot all of us go on a pilgrimage, Angog. We are not all of us married over to gods. Some of us still have to fasten our belts above something when we dress in the mornings."

"There is good pasture land," said Angog in a stiff, prickly way. "I hear some of the great warlords have their estates there and are ever in want of fresh blood in the herds."

"Blood. Always it is blood with you." The Chieftain was quiet for a long while. The young men sat by—Mylor among them, Indi saw—watching Cynr's face expectantly. Finally the young man sighed heavily and said, "Very well, we will leave this place and start afresh. There are fewer traders coming in anyway, and they say pirates are burning the coasts and coming farther and farther inland as they get bolder. May the gods be happy."

It did not dawn on Indi that they were really leaving until Cynr had dismissed his following and he stood on the porch of the houseplace, looking down to see Sillvia at the well with two of the other women. He looked at their familiar images and round the Downland hills and forests, and a wrench of deep-seeded love tore through his heart. "Oh, my runs," he whispered to the wind, lifting his face to feel the gentle beginnings of an autumnal shower. "Oh, my beautiful runs. To think you are only shadow things...to think I love you so much! How could there be a place more beautiful then here, held in the cradle of your arms? Hawthorn cream, chalk white, river blue, forest dark ... your colours, your whispers." He shook his head sadly. "I will carry you forever, wherever I go. And I will leave a part of me behind."

It was almost frightening how quickly they were all got together in the end and frightening how few there were to get. There were thin, straggly ponies heavy-laden with household treasures, the children, and the aged; sometimes a babe was strapped onto a hound's back. Indi himself carried Zeriah-rapha bound tightly to his chest, leading Cisha with Lenag astride her. Sillvia walked beside him, small and frail, but game as well. Her pale cheeks were flushing with the wind and determination.

They strung out like a grey tangle of wool along the lifting track, heading westward. None of them had a clear idea of how long it would take them, but for some reason they did not mind so much. A few cried on the last hill as the desolate remains of the old dun were lost to sight. Indi hugged the child and pushed on.

It took them two weeks to reach Woodhenge. It was in the centre of a thick pine wood, darker than a barrow now in the twilight that was falling as they arrived. Weary but glad to have the journey over with, they spread out around the big stockade, settling in amongst the natives with the usual difficulties. Claiming the presence of a priest, Cynr and his family were allowed residence in the hall. For a moment Indi wondered if that meant himself as well.

Standing in the gathering dusk, he looked round at the strangers, seeing himself as a stranger. The lord of the small dun was speaking to Cynr about higher matters; Indi did not pay much heed at present. He felt dwarfed by the towering old pines, ages older than the Red-Crests' eagles. Because of their closeness it shut out much of the light. There were spots of red glowing through the open doors of surrounding huts, beckoning gently to the chilled travellers.

"Rather uncanny," remarked a voice at his elbow, a voice that was not Sillvia's. Because of the dark and the foreign nature of the surroundings Indi had difficulty placing the voice and even jumped a little.

"Oh, Llyeln, it is only you," he breathed.

The younger man nodded. "It is I. Are we staying in the—" he pointed at the big wooden structure.

"I don't suppose we wouldn't," Indi mused. "For as much as he hates me, Cynr does seem to need me."

Llyeln glanced round at the huts. "Good. I should hate to sleep in a strange hut. Strange people snoring, strange dogs come a-licking at your face in the middle of the night. Strange girls … hmm …"

Indi cast him a withering look. Llyeln bent to fix his boot-laces, and they were saved from further discussion by the arrival of Tadc and Mylor.

"Where shall we bed, lord?" the former whispered.

Indi jerked at the title and looked round at his friend's face in the dark. But he saw it had come instinctively, not as a gesture for rebellion. He had never thought of rebellion himself.

"Not far from the building," he admonished. "See if you cannot board in the warriors' hall."

"Will do, lord." The two walked off.

Sillvia slipped her arm in Indi's and sighed. "We will not be here overlong," he told her. "Angog says this is only a brief stop. The winter, perhaps, and then we will be moving on in the spring."

Lenag lifted Zeriah-rapha out of her straps. "Thank goodness we will not be travelling in winter."

KIN-SLAYER

INDI TURNED HIS HEAD IN the thick forest moss to look at the still face beside him. He hated to wake her. After a long winter of living nearly on top of so many other people, it felt good to sleep in an open, quiet place. "Sillvia," he whispered. "Sillvia, wake up." She murmured and stirred softly, still too tired to answer. He crooked a smile. "Did I wear you out, dear?"

She murmured again and moved against him as a chill wind blew over them. The birds were singing and playing their afternoon songs: the gentle twitters from the pine boughs and cracklings in the fern beds. The sunlight came streaming gloriously down into the mossy forest. It filled the hollows with pools of gold. Everywhere there was a sense of peace and quiet with the whole wood breathing deeply as if in magic slumber. It was hard to be discontent. Indi whispered a prayer of thanksgiving and sank down again into the sylvan bed, cradling his wife in his arms. She was very warm and the wind had a little edge to it, so he pulled her close despite the warning in his head that they ought to return to Woodhenge soon.

"Are you all right?" he asked at length.

She stirred herself to answer now. "I am all right, lord," she whispered back. "Thank you."

"Do not thank me; I am a selfish man," Indi chuckled, running his big hands over her smooth warm skin. He took in her scent and lay back in the deep moss, watching her face. *God has given me so much,* he thought. *Despite the pain, I have been blessed.*

Sillvia winced and looked away, bringing his thoughts very much back to the present. "What is it?" he asked, sitting up sharply.

It took a while for her to answer him. She seemed to be wrestling with herself, fighting down an old jangling pain. "It is—" she began, and hesitated. "It is that I wish I had waited, that I had been faithful."

"You are," Indi replied sternly, but not without a great measure of gentleness. "Those days are far removed from you, wife, far removed in the blood of the Christos. And do not imagine I hold it against you; I don't. I don't ever think about it. I love you even more now than I did then."

She shook her head sorrowfully, holding on to him. The fire ran through him as he slid his hands behind her head. "You are so much like your God," she breathed. "Sometimes, when the light strikes you just so, I am afraid you *are* a God. You do not know what a horrible thing it is to lie with a God."

"Or a goddess," countered Indi with gravity. "As for the saints who are in the earth, they are the majestic ones in whom is all my delight."

"How is it that God loves me so much to give me Himself *and* you?" she murmured. "A loving God...!"

He quirked a smile, but before he could find some sort of answer, through the deep shadows and huge pale beams of sunlight, he heard a cry. At first it was too far off to hear clearly, then he could hear his pet name "Medi! Medi!" and he scrambled up. "It is Zeriah-rapha," he said. "What is she doing out here this far?" Instantly he pulled on his tunic and turned to Sillvia, who had sat up sharply when she heard the noise. "Don't worry, I will take care of her," he said.

"But if she should need comfort?" asked Sillvia concernedly.

"Come as soon as you are ready," replied Indi, striding off, "but don't tire yourself."

He jogged through the thick pine forest, following the child's voice and calling over to her in his deep, booming tones. Quickly he found her, standing at the top of a mossy rise, her little hands clasping two small trees beside her. She had grown into a thin, game little thing, full of her mother's beauty and her uncle's serious contemplation, toddling about at her games. There was little of her father in her.

Her face lit up the moment she saw Indi. He came to a stop below her, arms outstretched to catch her as she came skittering down. She was quite breathless. "What is it, cubling? Medi is here," he said gently, smoothing the brambles out of her hair.

The little girl pushed her hand under her nose and sniffed. "Medi," she said wearily, and put her face into his knees.

Indi ran his hands comfortingly through her tangled locks. She seemed spent, so that he guessed she had run from another of Angog's and her father's arguments—they were the worst sort of bedfellows, he reflected—and had come looking for him to comfort her. She brushed her nose against him, and he bent to lift her up. He straightened up just as Sillvia, dressed and quiet, came walking through the wood to meet them.

"What is going on?" she asked. "What was she doing this far out in the wood all alone?"

Indi hefted her up. "I think Cynr and Angog have been arguing again about moving on. Cynr must want to wait until after breeding season. But it is time we got back," he added. "The woods have a way of stealing your heart."

They tread up and down the lifting wooded hills until they got to the highest and looked down toward the east at the henge. The outlying village had grown since Indi's people had arrived, sprawling huts in the shadows of the pines, smelling of closeness and animals. As much as Indi thought it best to wait until after the breeding season, he thought he could not leave this dirty place quickly enough.

"I can smell supper," he remarked, nose to the wind.

They went down into the henge where Cunorix, lord of the dun, held his council and took his meat. The big man, half Saxon, was friendly enough, and his round, pine-wood hall had never been closed to them. But he was gone away with some of his retainers at present, which was well, for Cynr and Angog were once more going at it hammer and tongs.

Lenag was seated on a stool, her face drawn, her hands in her lap. She looked up as Indi entered and gave him a relieved smile as if she had been praying for his speedy return all this time. Zeriah-rapha ran into her arms and struggled up the front of her tunic. While Sillvia went off to help with the supper, Indi squatted down not too far from Cynr's chair and listened to the uproar between him and the priest.

"It's spring," Cynr was saying, very hard and precisely as though to get it into the other's head. "It's spring, and the stallions are going to be going for the mares. If I break off now, not only will I have the added danger of reckless stallions in a train, but I will likely lose a year's worth of foals. I can't afford that, Angog. *I can't afford that.* All the gods in hearing forgive me, but I can't sacrifice to lift a curse and at the same time sacrifice my people's livelihood!"

The sunlight filtering in through the open ceiling made dove-coloured shadows under the priest's robes as he paced. "You cannot see," he said in frustration. He went the length of the dais and returned. "You cannot see. Always it is the road in front of you, not the hill beyond it. Always what is in front of your face."

"That is because I am a man," said Cynr, "not a priest. If I tried to look beyond the next hill, my fields would rot at my back."

"And they do rot!" said Angog, whirling on one heel. "The whole body is filled with rot. How many of our people died over the winter? How many horses had to be sold for food? How many of the natives would as soon kill us as feed us? The blood is septic, Chieftain. It has to be let."

The Chieftain's brows clenched into darkness between his eyes. Through his teeth, he asked, "And why can it not be here?"

"And offer strange fire to the gods?" Angog countered.

There was a long moment of silence between the two, a silence almost tangible after the storm. Then, very gently and quietly, Cynr said, "Angog, priest to Tir, it is in my mind that the gods ask the wrong man to bloodlet for this curse. I will not rid us of one curse only to burden us with another."

"And if it is the only way?"

Again the silence. Where he sat, watching the eyes of the two, Indi felt his belly clench with urgency.

"I have yet to come round to your way of thinking," said Cynr.

Angog replied, "Must the whole dun die before you do? And meanwhile, let me do the thinking for you."

"I can do my own thinking for my own dun, and all that is mine to me! You know as well as I do that the gods roughly handle us when they handle us at all. The cure is as liable to kill us all as the illness. . . ." And he lapsed into a longer silence than before, brooding, arms draped across his knees, fingers idly twisting a length of straw as he stared into the fire. Indi did not like the look on his face, dark and almost malicious, confused, tense. It reminded him of the wolf he had baited in the cave.

Finally he jerked the piece of straw away and said, "We will leave before the breeding time. See to Indi."

See to Indi. In the periphery of his vision he had noticed the other men standing about, listening and, as Cynr spoke they came in, reaching for him. Out of instinct Indi leapt up, fists balled, ready to meet them. The overwhelming desire to live and the repulsion at being killed as a bloodletting for the dun propelled him backward out of the ring of young men, arms crossed in defence. There was a splutter of cries from the far side of the fire. A confusion of bodies came for him. He hit one man, felt the pain of it in his knuckles, and threw another across his hips.

There was a clear path. He lunged for it, only to bring the whole of Cynr's retainers on top of him. He went down with a crash among the hearthstones, the heat of the fire searing on his cheek. He gathered himself to jump upward, but one of them twisted his arms behind his back and pinned him to the ground. Panting, he knew it was all over.

Then the unthinkable happened. He remembered, afterward, how he had jerked his head out of the heat and ashes to see Cynr's hard-set face looking back at him, the look of one who has just done a hard thing and trying not to feel the sickness of it, the trying turning to unreasoning anger. Then out of the roaring in his ears he heard the pitiful cries of "Medi! Medi!" and he saw as one trapped in a dream Zeriah-rapha come running, Lenag snatching at her and missing as the child tried to reach him. He never knew afterward if she thought he was hurt or if she thought it was a game.

"Witch's brat!" cried Cynr, seeing her. Indi had not known until that moment that Cynr had it in him, but the man wrenched forward and brought a knife down through her skull with a crunch.

The body crumpled in a heap. Lenag screamed. With a rage he had never known until that moment, Indi erupted beneath his guards and flung himself over the child's body. It hung listless in his arms, tiny, pale like a little white flower with the sun behind it. He pulled his head up from her hair, shielding her with his own body, his face splattered in her blood. "Kin-slayer!" he yelled. "*Kin-slayer!*"

And Cynr, who was drunk with anger by now, got to his feet, very still and white. "I could never know she was mine and not yours. If the dun is to be bloodlet, then it will be bloodlet."

He struggled toward Cynr, not thinking about what he did. But arms held him back, and even as he swung to fight, something struck him on the back of the head and the lights went out.

He came to himself in darkness, only knowing he had awoken because of the pain in his head. For a while he lay on his belly on a dirt floor, pulling in heavy breaths, flanks heaving like those of a small hunted animal. His mind was dazed. His throat was raw, as though he had been yelling. There was a burning sickness in his chest. Why was his head thundering? Why did his chest and throat feel as though he had been retching out his heart?

Through the confusion he managed to remember pieces of the hellish scenes from Cunorix's hall. He groaned and rolled over, red stars spangling his vision, to stare up helplessly through the darkness. He wondered where Lenag was, and Sillvia, and if anyone would see to the child. He remembered his sister's scream, like a coney caught in a snare; he quickly brushed aside the horror of it.

Kin-slayer. He gingerly pulled himself up to a sitting position and propped himself against the wall of his little prison. Over and over he saw Cynr snapping forward, the knife glittering as it passed through a patch of sunlight, coming away spitting red. A part of him tried to assure him it had been a nightmare, that it had not been real. He would wake up soon; perhaps it was the long winter and he had been ill, and presently he would come out of the illness and the evil dreams.

Cynr had always had it in him, he reasoned. He shook his head wearily, lightning lancing across his vision. He had sold his dog, which he had raised from a pup, for a bow; he had stood in the way when Angog came to offer Sitag up in return for her father's life. What was it to him that a child died, a child whom he suspected was not his own? In a detached sort of way, as though it mattered, he wondered what morning it had been in which Cynr had woken up and found he believed his own lies.

There was a rattle at the latch. Indi swung round, pulling his legs beneath himself. But when the door opened the light came in, blinding him, stabbing his brain like daggers. He flung his hands over his face and groaned.

"*Aiyah*, it will be hurting," said a familiar voice. He heard the door shut and blinked to find Tadc-Hound coming to squat down beside him, a lamp in one hand and a bowl of gruel in the other. "Take the bowl. I will see to your head."

"Are they not suspecting you?" asked Indi, surprised to find how heavy and woollen his tongue felt in his mouth. He took the bowl and bent his head over it as Tadc prodded at the lump on the back of his head.

"They are not suspecting me," Tadc replied absentmindedly. "I have taken care that they should not, for your sake."

He asked after Lenag and Sillvia, particularly Sillvia, whose absence he was feeling keenly.

"I took Sillvia to Llyeln, who will keep her well enough and out of harm's way, least suspicious of us all as he is. She was as beside herself for you as Lenag was for the cubling. She is a vixen, your little woman. She would have flung herself at Cynr's throat as you had, had Mylor not been there to stop her."

Tadc's hands worked over the back of his head, increasing the hammer-thunder. Indi sat under the surgery and ate his gruel, feeling at the end of it as though he would retch it all back up again. But somehow he managed to keep it down. He wanted to ask about Zeriah-rapha but thought he might lose his handle on reality, which was already slipping a bit due to the pain in his head, so he moved on. "When are we going to Angog's temple of stone?"

"Soon." The fellow rocked back on his heels, finished with his inspection. "They are afraid you will run and that the gods will be angry forever, and so they want to kill you as soon as may be." He lapsed into a sullen quiet, then added, "Is there anything I can do for you, my lord?"

It took Indi a moment to answer. Through the muddle that the blow had left his mind, he tried to form a plan. "When we come to this temple of stone," he said presently, slowly, "I need Mylor to stay with Lenag, and I need you to take Sillvia to Yr Widdfa. There is a friend there, Procyon."

"I remember him, lord."

The next part was hard in coming out. His raw throat clenched. "I need you to look after her when I am gone. Care for her. She is a good woman. One of the finest."

Tadc gripped his shoulder hard. "We will name the first son after you."

He left then, taking the light and the bowl with him, leaving Indi to a deeper and quieter desolation than he had felt before.

The Long Dark

It was an easy road to the henge of stone. The land about was open country, good for crops, with quarries for stone to make the doorways of the houses that would be put up. The rest of the dun was glad to be out of their cramped quarters and eager to be carving a new village out of the empty territory.

Indi watched their work from a distance, sullen and quiet, feeling oddly detached from it all. They chained him up, often to a tree like a dog, when he was not locked away in a shed for the night to be sure he did not bolt. And he wanted to bolt. He wanted to run, to take Sillvia away to join Procyon and be free. But he knew he would not be free, and he would be wearing the gall of the thrall-ring all his days. Sitting with his back to his tree in the smothering heat, listening to a stallion go for a mare and the shouts of the men keeping the violence to a minimum, he reflected on obedience unto death, and though he knew his could not compare to the sorrows his Lord bore, he understood it was a bitter, bitter drink to down, and his stomach clenched at the thought.

He could only hope that God would give him the strength to face the long dark barrow without flinching. "Oh God," he whispered into the hollow night. "I need you in this dark hour."

A shadow fell across his lap, and he looked up as the figure paused to see Llyeln looking down at him. "Oh," he said wearily. "It is you." And he noticed without really seeing that the young man had begun to darken about the cheeks, finally beginning to grow a bit of fuzz. He reached up absentmindedly and brushed the back of his hand over his chin, feeling the roughness that met him.

"And it is you," said Llyeln, and Indi heard the desolation in the other's tone.

They fell silent. The mare was squealing somewhere, and the wind blowing through the hawkbit around Indi's feet brought the sound of hooves on the hard turf.

Suddenly Llyeln jerked his arms across his chest, crossing them tightly. "Can't you run, Indi?" he blurted out. "I can break the chain. You can find a smith somewhere to file off the ring. You *can't* just sit there and let them do this to you!"

"I can, and I must," Indi replied. "They are killing me for my faith, and what can a man do but stand and take it? I could not live with myself if I ran."

The other dropped into an angry, brooding silence. Indi hoped he would not go on, not trusting himself to hold firm to his own conviction, to drink the whole cup dry. But Llyeln did not go on. He stooped with a violent, kingfisher gesture and plucked up a head of yellow hawkbit, turning it over and over in his hands. He was pulling off a piece of the flower with each turn. When it was no more than a broken bud of green, he threw it away. "You're a better man than I, Indi," he said. And he turned on his heel and walked away, leaving Indi alone again.

But he was only alone for an hour before two Cynr's men came down from the new hall and unchained him from the tree. They handled him roughly, and while he wanted to ask them what the urgency was, he knew he would only get a strike across the jaw for speaking. So he walked with them up the muddy track toward the huddle of huts that had been erected. It was not until they pushed him into his confinement cell that he realized what the trouble was.

Tadc and Sillvia were both there before him, the former seated on the ground, his head laid across his arms, the latter pacing the room. She turned as the door was swung open and was running into his arms as the door was shut after him.

"Sillvia!" he said huskily. "What—how did you—why are you not—"

"They caught us," Tadc said mournfully into his arms. "I thought it best to leave before tonight, to give us a good head start." He pulled his head out of his arms. "I took Sillvia with me into the woods, enough food for a few days in my pack. But it seems I was not careful enough, and Cynr is too suspicious. We had gone only a morning's walk before his whelps caught up to us and brought us back."

Touching his tongue to his suddenly dry lips, Indi nodded. They would all die now, he considered. *At least … at least Sillvia will not have to live without me*, he thought.

"I tried, lord."

He shook his head, dismissing Tadc's failure. He put his face down in Sillvia's tangled hair, holding her close as she tried to press herself as near to him as she could manage. He had not seen her or held her since the day Zeriah-rapha had died. Perhaps it was only a week ago—he had lost count of the days—but it seemed so long, so far away. And the nightmare was not over.

He lifted her up and sank down beside Tadc, holding her in his arms. She was shaking, afraid, but she managed to not cry. Tadc put his head back on his arms, and Indi held his wife until the shaking subsided and she had dropped off into a fitful sort of sleep, twitching now and then.

"Indi?"

He turned his head. "Yes, Tadc?"

The other man's tattoos showed up sharply in the light that came in through the high crack above the door. "I'm glad I'm dying with you."

"And you," Indi replied, and he found that he meant it.

The day dragged by. Indi slept as fitfully as Sillvia when he could sleep. Tadc rose and paced at times, but for the most part they remained silent, content in each other's company. A lark trilled outside once, and when a nightingale answered, Indi looked up to see the light in the crack over the door had turned to steely grey, and he knew it was gathering toward evening.

Shortly after that there came a harsh knock which shook the door on its flimsy hinges, and the same two guards stepped in. One held a basin full of water, the other carried a bundle of clothing under one arm.

"Wash and dress," the first one said as the second tossed the bundle over. "Knock when you are ready to come out."

They left, locking the door behind them. Sillvia held the bowl for Indi as he put down the bundle and got out of his dirty tunic.

"Indi, I'm frightened," Sillvia whispered, holding the towel for her lord.

Indi stared into the washing bowl, his reflection nearly invisible in the water. Words of hollow comfort were on his lips when something struck him. "Sillvia," he said, pointing. "Sillvia, look at the water. What do you see?"

She brushed her finger beneath her nose and obeyed him quietly, looking down at the surface between them. "I see your hand," she replied after a pause, eyes flickering to his. "And I see your face too, a little."

"But not very well?"

"No, not very well."

He let out a heavy breath. "That is what we are like, sweet. We are only shadows, ghosts on this plain. If I die at sunset tomorrow, I will be free of this shadow and all the shadows of this world. I will be before the Real."

"Is this pain not real?" Sillvia's eyes swam.

He reached across the bowl and tipped her chin up. "It is real, and great, but it is only part of the shadow things. It will pass with the Morning. The sunset may be our morning."

She nodded wordlessly. He washed and let Tadc have the honour of dressing him in the scarlet tunic and bronze-worked ceremonial belt. It was very old, the metal around the pin eaten with verdigris, and he wondered how many people had died before him wearing this belt. But at least he would not be a disgrace. He stood up straight as Tadc pulled the belt's clasp dead-centre around his middle, watching Sillvia as she watched him.

"How is it?" he asked.

She attempted a smile. "You look very fine. Like a chieftain's son."

"You are ready, lord," said Tadc.

Since this would be the last time he would have a moment with her alone, Indi pulled Sillvia close and kissed her, tasting her salty tears on her lips. Only for a moment he pulled in the scent and feel of her one last time then wrenched away and met the door with his fist.

It shuddered under the blow, and in a moment the latch was rattling, drowning out Sillvia's uncontrollable little sob, and Indi was ducking out between his guards into the dusk.

The twilight had descended very quietly. Bats whirled above the little dun, hovering between the soft smudged columns of smoke rising from the fireholes in the roofs. A pony whinnied.

One of his guards took his arm, but he said softly, "I can walk alone," and after a hard look into the other's eyes, he was released. He went up between them under the steely grey evening sky, barred in the west with its hints of gold and primrose, to the Chieftain's hall. The dogs at the door got up and snarled with their lips curled back to red, scrabbling back as they passed through.

There was quite a gathering in the hall. Indi stood uncertainly in the doorway, looking down the raw new hearthfires at the groups of retainers and ladies, food and mead—and Cynr. He sat at the head of the throng in his boarskin chair, hunched over a little. His body seemed frail though the power he still possessed burned wildly in his eyes. Flickering, those eyes rose to Indi's. The eyebrows shot up, surprised and almost admiring. The Chieftain beckoned with a finger.

Indi crossed the hall, drawing the glances of the others. He felt rather than saw the presence of Angog in the shadows, wrapped up in all his dark holiness. And beyond Cynr he saw Lenag standing rigid, pale, her face hollow as if she had been crying. He looked at her once, pointedly, wishing all the power of God upon her.

The young slave stopped still before the Chieftain, hands clenched at his sides, booted feet stock in their place. Cynr regarded him for a moment in silence, that familiar tic of anger pulling at one brow. Without looking, Indi was aware of the other rubbing a thumb against a forefinger, thoughtfully.

"You set Tadc-Hound against me," the Chieftain said at last. His tone was low, easy, almost nonchalant. He glanced aside into the burning depths of the fire. "You set Tadc-Hound, *my* Hound, against me, and set him off with your wife. Or do I have my condolences to offer you in the little time you have left, and was it your wife who went off with Tadc?"

The words struck Indi like spears of straw off stone. Cynr's words in his ears were a distant droning, distinct and yet meaningless. He was about to die. He was about to be stretched out on a cold stone altar and have a knife driven through the hollow of his neck. What could Cynr say that would compare with that?

Seeing that his words had no effect, Cynr went on. "Angog assures me that killing you for the sake of the dun is sacrifice, not kin-slaying. And I am willing to let him take you. You were a good dog, up until the last. But I won't miss you."

Indi came to himself. "Have a care," he replied. "You do not know the horror you bring upon yourself with my death. I am a son of God, and he does not take lightly those who profane His name and ill-use His people. Have a care."

"I have had enough of your God!" Cynr said, lashing out a hand. "He is not my God, nor is He God here, and He has caused nothing but trouble for my people. Angog will kill you and silence once and for all your voice and your God's."

"My quarrel," replied Indi, "is not with you, Cynr. I will go to Stonehenge with Angog. I will confront this god of yours in the name of my own, and we will see, either now or beyond our deaths, which is the true and powerful ruler of all."

Behind them Lenag let out a small moan, hand clasped to her mouth.

"You!" Cynr spun around and pointed with two fingers at her. "Yes, you weep. You will go with your brother, you witch. I cannot trust you any longer."

It was then that Cynr's words touched him. "No!" Indi cried, starting forward, but the men leapt up on all sides to hold him back and to arrest Lenag.

Cynr showed his teeth. "You can trust your life to your God, but you cannot trust Lenag's? What a hypocrite you are, slave. No, Angog has permission to bloodlet this dun and rid it of this fever."

Letting out a low, savage growl, Indi bunched his arms and wrenched free of his captor's grasp to catch Lenag as the men pushed her to Indi's side. When they tried to haul her away, and when she let out a little cry of pained protest, he swung out a balled fist at her guard and struck him in the face, hurling the man back and bringing her firmly to his side in a protective gesture.

"I may be a slave," Indi told them, and Cynr, who had come to his feet, "but harm this woman and I will die here, now, bringing as many of you down with me as I may!"

"Take them out!" Cynr emptied his drinking horn at them violently, and he stalked away, hefting his great cloak around his shoulders as he went.

The men ushered them out into the heavy darkness, cruel but careful not to rouse Indi's ire. He kept his hand firmly above Lenag's elbow, helping her along in the night. The firelight guttered behind them as the doorflap fell to. Their guards seemed content to hold them in the forecourt of the raw new hall, waiting for the other offerings to be brought and for the rest of the dun to assemble.

Suspecting that he would only bring mischief upon them if he tried to comfort Lenag, who was standing very still with her head up and her chin set firmly, he turned and looked up at the stars. They scattered across the heavens as though God had thrown a fistful of silver on the black. They were beautiful and steadying too, for a little fear of death had come joggling most unpleasantly at his elbow when Cynr had condemned Lenag to the same fate. *Shadow things*, he told himself. *This time tomorrow—this time tomorrow, we will be in eternity.*

Presently the drums began. They started distantly at first, as if they were miles away and over vast hills, coming slowly on the wind toward them, but they grew in strength, the boom low and baleful in the air. In the pale light of the stars Indi looked round to see the others, Tadc and Sillvia, being brought up by Mylor to join them. He did not speak a word to them, but he reached out and took Sillvia's hand—Tadc slipped in and put a hand on Lenag's elbow to keep her steady over the dark terrain—and he felt a sort of quiet, unearthly fellowship snake between them all that he was certain no other people would experience.

The drums were echoing over the entire dun and were joined with the pound of many feet. Torches flickered before the huts. Men with their women and children tagging along filed out, grouping in front of the Chieftain's hall. There seemed to be a great many of them, bunched and shifting as they were, torchlight sputtering and flickering over their heads. There was a wave-like wailing going back and forth through the gathering, taken up mostly by the women. The sound of it made Indi's skin crawl with coldness.

There was a parting near the far end of the crowd—the wailing continued—and through the ranks a low, open-fronted chariot came, pulled by two fine black ponies. Cynr gripped the bronze-worked rail by the driver, and Angog stood just behind him. The ponies bounded down the hillside, bringing the chariot rumbling after, and the driver bent back on the reins to bring it to a halt between Indi and his people, and the crowd.

Angog changed places at the side of the chariot and leaned toward Indi. There was a bowl in one hand, and he dipped his thumb into what was in it and drew a damp line across Indi's brow. His jaw tightened, every inch of his will straining away from the mark of blood. "Bow," Angog commanded when he had finished.

The young man looked from the one to the other between the trickle of blood: the priest decked out in white, which was now orange from the glow of torches, and the Chieftain clad in his best. Putting his shoulder toward the priest, he bowed from the waist to the Chieftain.

A blow sent a burst of stars across his vision. Who had delivered it, Indi did not know; he heard Sillvia give a little cry behind him, but he picked himself up of his own accord and stood again before Cynr and Angog. "Why do you strike me?" he asked.

Cynr's face was impassive, but Indi could feel a small glimmer of confusion behind those eyes, and he knew the other was confounded by his show of fealty. Angog bristled. "Bow before the gods," he said, his voice even deeper than usual. "Bow before your lords and makers."

The whole crowd was hushed, eyes bent on the rigid figure by the Chieftain's chariot. "I will never bow before you or your gods," Indi replied quietly, feeling those eyes on him. "I have given my allegiance to the Lord of heaven now, and he is my Maker. How can I go back on Him?"

Before Angog could reply, Cynr held out his hand. "Let the knife decide, priest." He turned back to regard Indi. "You should know this slave of mine well enough to realize that once he has set his hand to a thing, he will not be turned back. Let our gods break his stubborn spine, and let us be rid of it. Drive on."

The wail went up on all sides again as the driver whipped up the ponies and they began to move out of the dun for the plain. Walking with the rest, hedged in by the guards, Indi told himself, *These are the shadow things. Take courage. The stars will still shine tomorrow, and you will shine the brighter ere this night draws to an end. These are the shadow things. Take heart.*

The chariot rattled down the slope between the houses, following the sweep of the low hills toward the raised plateau that the huge stone monument rested on. Facing the east, it was a dark lump against the skyline, like the heavy crown of a stone giant that lay on the land. The horizon burned with a lowering gold light, bringing up the distant woods black and ragged against the sky. As the torchlit procession made its way down to the plain and across its wide breadth, the stars began to come out, one by one then two by two, and then, with a silent burst, a countless array sparkled in the heavens, untouched by the tumult below. Bats wheeled between them, following the invisible lines from one pin-point to the next, darting in lost, erratic circles in the air.

Watching them, moving with the pulsing crowd, Indi thought how very like them the dun-people were: coming out only at night yet searching from star to star for some light for their sightless eyes, wheeling in the blackness, yelping for a path to follow.

Stonehenge neared. Above the torches Indi could see its stones rising higher and higher as they marched up the long avenue between the ditches. The pack fanned out, spreading round on the outskirts of the largest ring of trilithons, their voices silenced. In a small group, Indi and his people stood between their guards, waiting for the call to move forward. There seemed to be no time, only stars and torches and the stones black against the darkness.

A horn shrilled. The priest got down and moved forward, and the guards brought Indi and the others with them. Through the ranks of stones they passed, walking into the inner circle. The scent of oppressive evil overhung the place.

Faces showed up faintly in the light. Eyes shone, blinking, glimmering back at him. In the surrealism of the moment, the slave thought he would wake soon from the dream. But as he thought this, one of the chariot ponies let down its hoof with a mighty stamp, and the image of little Zeriah-rapha crumpling under the knife lashed through his mind, bringing the blood pounding to his light head.

Eyes shining with a brightness unlike the torchlight, Indi turned to Cynr in the chariot. The Chieftain was descending, still thin and limping a little from the long effects of the famine yet bearing himself regally and with pride, dressed in the glamour of a dun-lord. He looked across at Indi, noting the glance, and raised his brows questioningly. For a moment there was something of the old Cynr in there, something of the friendly young man who had been his companion through the years before Procyon. Then

Procyon, and the cross, and the Christos came between them, and the veil was pulled across the Chieftain's eyes again.

Watching the Chieftain and Angog set themselves at the farthest corners of the altar, he thought, *This is what Sitag faced, the long dark and the knife's glint. This is what she faced without any hope. Ah, God! Receive Your son tonight. I and mine will be with You beyond the shadow things ere the dawn comes.*

Strong arms took Indi and bound his arms behind his back, leaving his mouth and legs free. The pride he was born with resented the cords, yet he bore them, somehow, with grace. He would be happy to share the shame of the Christos.

Then the ceremony began. The crowd set up the wailing and a chant, and the torches were thrust into a pile of faggots that had been set up earlier. With a spurt, barely heard because of the crowd's noise, the fire took and sprang into the air, blotting out a great deal of the stars. In the language of the gods the priest began his own maledictions and pleas, droning long through incantations that would free the dun from the curse when Indi was killed. Indi shut his eyes, sinking into his heart of hearts where he prayed through the noise, through the hours that went on. He wished dearly they would kill him and be done with it. He stood rigid, quiet, praying in his heart for peace as the stars wheeled on beyond the smoke.

SCARLET DAWN

FINALLY THE MOMENT CAME. ANGOG gave a barking order and the guards converged around Indi. Now that the moment had arrived, Indi could taste fear at the back of his throat. The hands that pulled him now felt like the claws of birds. *God, God, this is a horrible death!* he thought desperately. *Do not let me lose heart now!*

Toward the altar he was taken, pushed and prodded unnecessarily. He was set up on the little raised bit of earth across the stone slab from Cynr, and looking at the Chieftain's face again, Indi felt the whirling world steady a bit.

"It is too late to take it all back now," Cynr said through his teeth.

Indi shook his head. "I would not take it back, even so."

Lifting his brows, the Chieftain nodded. "But you are about to meet the gods, Indi," he said. "Have you not even a little fear of them?"

He had to be honest. "Cynr Once-Brother," he replied, standing still as Angog approached, "I would be a fool not to fear those who still hold you in their sway. But my God is far greater and His sacrifice is by far a more excellent thing than my own. It is because of *that* death that I do not despair now and that I have a hope of life beyond."

"May the gods obliterate your memory from the earth," Angog told him. A long knife, hilted with the horn of a ram, glittered in his fist. With a nod from him Indi was grabbed round the waist and legs and hoisted up onto the slab, laid so that he was looking up into the darkness, through the smoke, at the stars. Cords were wrapped around his knees and ankles so that he would not get away should he try to bolt before the knife came down.

Angog moved to his side, whispering under his breath. Again the scent of darkness emanated from him, but Indi knew well by now this was the unholy smell of all evil things. It burned in his nostrils.

The priest leaned over him; in the waiting silence, Indi thought he could hear a woman's weeping. With small bright eyes, the priest said, "Now we will at last end this quarrel, and our dun will be free of the famine that you have set it under."

A stillness flowed through Indi's body, an indescribable sensation that came from neither himself nor the world he inhabited. "My quarrel is not with you, Angog," he told the priest gently. "Do what you will; you have God to answer to."

Setting his hand on Indi's collarbone, Angog raised the knife high into the air. That old, gnarled hand did not shake: its experienced knuckles turned white from the grip; the calculating eyes honed in on the spot the knife would plunge through.

A whistle broke the air. Angog dropped—Indi winced as the knife came down, cutting his arm—gurgling onto the stone slab, slipping off the edge. Confused screams rent the air. Unable to move, Indi could not tell what was afoot. In the turmoil Cynr let out a cry of despair and lunged toward the crumpled priest, ripping the knife out of his grasp. Turning to Indi, he snarled, "I will not give up my dun, not for all the gods in the heavens, not for all the brotherhoods in the world!" And he lifted the knife himself.

The whistle came again. Cynr was too late in his blow, and this time Indi saw the arrow come through the man's neck with a spray of crimson. He heard Lenag's scream. Coughing up a little surprised burst of blood, the Chieftain dropped the knife and clawed at his throat, falling out of Indi's vision upon the ground; he could hear him kicking and gurgling as Angog had done.

The area was thrown into a panic. Women screamed, men shouted; a child began to cry as one of the ponies whinnied madly. In his falling throes Cynr had spat blood across Indi's face, and it felt horribly warm and ticklish on his cheek. But through the upheaval a familiar voice sent up a savage cry.

"Away from him! Away from him, you brutes, or I will shoot you where you stand!"

Llyeln! The lifeblood pounded through Indi's body in such a heady wave he thought it would blot out his reason. Was he not to die after all? Was he to live? What was happening?

There was a confused space of noise in which the people murmured and the warriors seemed to mill around, darting forward and back, wanting to reach their priest and fallen Chieftain yet afraid of the apparently invisible assailant. They did not know if it was a god or a man, but until they found out they chose not to test him further.

The voice came again. "Untie him! Harm him, and I will drop you dead where you stand!"

Mylor came forward and hastily undid the ropes around Indi. Stiffly he got up, panting a little, trying to take stock of his surroundings. There Angog and Cynr lay, quite dead, arrows through their back and neck. The knife was presumably crushed underneath them, for he did not see it. The crowd was keeping back, terrorized to a hush. His little band clumped against the nearest trilithon, waiting anxiously to see what happened next.

"Stand away!" Llyeln said from his hiding place among the dark. "Stand away! You—driver! Give your Chieftain his spear!"

The ponies tossed their heads as the driver cautiously took out his spear. Instantly Tadc came forward, wrenching the spear from the man's hands, and stepped out across the enclosure, head up, eyes gleaming. Grateful, Indi took the weapon from him, giving the man a small smile and a quick clasp of the shoulder. Tadc bowed a little and stepped back.

Brandishing his spear, Indi called into the dark, "Come forward and show yourself!"

There was a little pause, then in the dark there came a heavy thump, and out of the darkness Llyeln walked, carrying Cynr's loaded bow, eyes darting round to be sure no one jumped him. He had scaled a stone and stood upon the top where he could clearly see all that went on below and at the opportune moment, weighing the price of one death for the price of another, had shot down both the priest and then the Chieftain before the fateful blow could be struck.

Before Indi he stopped and sank to one knee, ducking his head. "Hail, my Chieftain," he murmured.

Indi got down off the altar and quietly lifted the little Roman-British half-breed to his feet, gazing into his eyes. He was suddenly sad; his brows drew together in contemplation. "Why did you do it, Llyeln?" he asked softly. His hand trembled a little on the other's forearm. "Why did you raise your arm against another man?"

Llyeln's eyes hardened into brittle orbs, and his jawline became sharper. "You once told me," he said, "in the quiet hours during the winter, of a man who slew his younger brother out of jealousy before the face of God. I was not about to let that transpire again."

With a physical jab of pain Indi's heart seemed to break into a thousand shimmering pieces. "Oh, Llyeln!" he cried, and embraced the other tightly. He could feel the pressure of the thrall-ring against his neck, the other's strong hands clasping his upper arms in the desperate gesture one gives to something one has almost lost.

Other hands gripped him. Turning, Indi found himself surrounded by Sillvia, Lenag, Tadc, and Mylor. Their crying, laughing, amazed faces seemed to swim around him as he reached for them all, drawing them in. Someone cried, "Praise God, He is good!" and he could not agree more. The pound of life inside his head was very great. The scent of death and the world beyond was removed, and he found he could breathe again, though even in that moment he realized that it would come again, though perhaps not under the knife. But it would surely come, and the scent of death would give way to the aroma of the higher world, the splendour and the glory of heaven.

Thrall-ringed, Indi turned to the crowd. The two women stood off at a little distance, chins tipped in British pride, eyes aglow. The men gathered round Indi. "People," the young man called, "make your decision now: your Chieftain is dead. I am the son of your old Chieftain: will you take me, or will you go your own way back to your dun and elect another man to govern you?"

Within their faces Indi could see a strain of uncertainty. Their traditions pulled them strongly in the direction of a Chieftain's son, but not so easily could they forget the curse that had ravished their crops in two years. So they pushed forward one man, who replied, "We will elect another man. Do you go, and do not trouble us anymore."

Indi nodded. "So. But you will not leave us destitute nor turn us out like stray dogs. Give us a third of my father's herd and food enough for several days, and then you will be free of us."

Eager to be free of them, some of the men and the boys went off to do as Indi bid, and as the men moved to gather up their dead leaders, Tadc slipped up beside Indi.

"What is in your mind, lord?"

Watching the men pick the limp body of Cynr up, oddly feeling no remorse, as though the body were but a straw-stuffed image, he heard himself reply, "We will make a northward droving and find the place men call Yr Widdfa. There is a place at a hearthfire there for me and mine, and Procyon will be there, waiting for me."

"So." Tadc nodded. "It is a good plan."

Presently Mylor came back to him to say that the women wanted to gather their things before they set out. Indi let him go, finding the mantle of Chieftainship fell easily about his shoulders. There would be enough between the two women to load several ponies, he considered. And there must be some piece of finery among Lenag's things to make a present to Lord Bedwyr.

He touched the thing round his neck, feeling the coldness and the warmth of it and the heaviness too. That was not something easily confined to the past with the bolt of a bow. Underneath it he could feel the gall the iron had left and knew its telltale sign would be there forever. It was a bittersweet victory.

The crowd was beginning to dissipate, many of them following the dead Chieftain and priest back toward the dun, wailing as they went. He watched them go and, with a little jolt, saw his mother among them. Brows furrowed, he asked as she came near, "Will you come with us, Mara?"

The woman started at the name, drawing up like a struck bird. Indi saw her eyes harden for a moment, then, with a cold shake of her head, she said, "I do not know you, young man. You pretend to be my son, but I buried my son long ago in the barrowed hills."

Indi could only watch her leave in stately dignity, her dress sweeping through the short turf as she made her way back toward the dun.

It was indeed a bittersweet victory.

The sky was turning a rusty blue by the time the sound of hooves filled the air. With the stars winking out, the east touched with marigold, and the turf turning a burnished green, a third of the herd was turned out for him to see: fine, hardy native ponies with strains of Roman blood in them, some of them carrying their tails remarkably high, showing good breeding. That, he thought, would make a good gift to Lord Bedwyr. With the first breath of the water-cool dawn wind whipping across the plain, Llyeln joined him as they approached the herd, ready to mount up and make the northward droving to Yr Widdfa.

Indi glance aside at his younger friend. "Are you coming with me?" he asked.

"Need you ask that, lord?" replied Llyeln with a look of reproach. The young Chieftain pulled a smile. No, he need not ask. Llyeln would always be there for him, of that he was certain. But then he added, "To whom *would* I go? I think a living God is with you," which gave the cold morning a certain touch of warmth to Indi.

As they passed out through the stones down the grassy avenue, something caught the light of the advancing sun and shone a moment. Llyeln bent down and Indi paused to see what it was. The young man turned up in his hand a smoothly polished stone, very flat on one side: an archer's cuff. It must have slipped off Cynr's wrist as they carried him away. There was a little space of stillness between them as they looked at it, but when Llyeln raised his brows indicatively, Indi shook his head. The other shrugged and tossed it underhanded away into the trench. They walked away and let it tumble, shining in the red light, to fall among the yellow hawkbit, forgotten.

GLOSSARY

Ancasta: a Celtic goddess.

Downs: an area of low, open chalk hills.

Dun: a village or settlement.

Gaul: modern-day France.

Map: meaning 'son of'.

Red-Crests: a term for the Romans, specifically their military, whose officers wore helmets with red plumes.

Stonehenge: a pagan ring of stone used as a temple.

Taranis: a Celtic god of thunder.

Tir: a war-god carried over from Germanic peoples.

Venta (Bulgarum): modern-day Winchester, Hampshire.

Woodhenge: a pagan ring of wood used as a temple.

Yr Widdfa: Snowdon Mountain in northern Wales.

For more information about Jennifer,
please visit her website:

www.thepenslayer.blogspot.com

If you enjoyed *The Shadow Things* please check out Jennifer's sister, Abigail J. Hartman, and her historical fiction, *The Soldier's Cross*.

1415 A.D.

Fiona's world is a carefully built castle in the air, made up of the fancies, wishes, and memories of her childhood. It begins to crumble as she watches her brother march away to join in the English invasion of France. It falls to pieces when he is brought home dead.

Robbed of the one dearest to her and alone in the world, Fiona turns to her brother's silver cross in search of the peace he said it would bring. But when she finds it missing, she swears she will have it and sets out on a journey across the Channel and war-ravaged France to regain it and find the peace it carries.